# The Diamond

# Scalpel

First paperback edition February 2020

*Cover Designed by Julie Horino*

ISBN 978-0-578-64700-5 (paperback)

Letter from your Friendly Neighborhood Writer:

*Thank you so much for your purchase and support of my 2<sup>nd</sup> novel **The Diamond Scalpel.***

*The world in this story is a lot like the twilight zone, another time another dimension. It is a world similar but different than our own. I hope you enjoy.*

*I'd like to give a special shout out to Guy McCloskey for his professional eye and encouragement on my first novel **The Press Secretary**. Also, thank you to the magnificent team of Gokuren Publishing: Julie Horino, Monica Horino, Cyle Colbert, Mose Henderson, Robert Arnold, and my childhood neighbor Will. You wouldn't be holding this book without them.*

*4/10/2020*

# The Diamond Scalpel

By Stanley Ish

GOKUREN PUBLISHING
2020

*Once again to my Mushroom.*

# Chapter One:
## Champagne Problems

A non withstanding day provoked the matter…as chance should snap us back to realities point with a missing link that begins our story.

VLADIMIR FORTUNE stepped forth from the prison gates. A great treasures worth of delight sprayed from NIKI BROWN and her cousin, ALAIN MACHADO, as they saw Vladimir for the first time in ten years. His hair had grown long hanging down his face. As he nodded, thanks to the guards he had come to know well, Vladimir took a long deep breath of free fresh air. His lungs filled to the brim with the exhilaration of the life left for him to live. Exhaling out all the doubts and worries plaguing society, Vladimir Fortune took the first steps of his twentieth life.

The drive from the prison into town was quiet while both Niki and Alain waited for Vladimir's cue, one he chose not to give as they rode to the company home. The silence between the three grew thick as the wheels rolled down the highway. Vladimir watched the trees wave by as his mind drifted into the past as a cacophony of thoughts rained down a toxic blanket of pain.

The fact of the matter was that Vladimir was now nowhere safe--using his nineteenth life to put movements into play for a ceasefire that should have never been delayed. "How had it all gotten so out of hand," Vlad thought as the car pulled onto the grounds of Sector 4 of Company 23.

Somewhere in the late 2020's when the earth began to split apart, the fifty states of America went up for sale and were bought by the top fourteen companies making up the majority of power in the world. These companies stripped the names of all 50 states and replaced them with numbers; California became to be known as Company 23.

Sector 4 was what used to be Culver City, the once bustling home of MGM studios and the center of action during the great golden age of cinema. When Vlad stepped out of the vehicle, Niki and Alain picked him up from prison with their familiar smell of the old neighborhood wafting back to him.

Growing up poor has never been fashionable. There were never any kids looking up to Oliver Twist because he was a poor kid. No, it was his wit and courage that conned the hearts of nineteenth century children and adults. Poverty, the ever present facet swimming throughout Charles Dickenson's bibliography was not glorified to be sought, nor chased to be tackled upon unexpectedly. While handed out wealth and opportunity grace few, the rest have it ripped away.

Vladimir Fortune was born at the beginning of his family's ripening. Three generations before him, the Fortune family had grown epically, achieving great notoriety reserved only for those cut from a cloth of excellence that could only be obtained through the expensive instruction of The Grape family.

The grape family, as you are aware, maintained a status of superiority for generations. When the great auction of the fifty states occurred, it was the Grape family that acquired the majority of states up to sale. They quickly sold them off and the 50 companies were created. It could be said that the Grapes are the glue holding this great nation of ours together.

Vladimir looked at himself in the mirror once he was back in his old room in the third floor of the company home. Each day he had ticked off his sentence in that dirty concrete cell. Each of those days were etched completely into him. A never-ending barrage of feeling, heavy thick feeling, pulled from within him. There was nothing to be done about it. Staring back at eyes he barely recognized, Vlad smiled at the absurdity of being on his 20th life.

◆ ◆ ◆

"I'm not even sure how to explain the 20 life concept," Vlad thought to himself as he lathered his face with shaving cream. Taking his time shaving with his left hand, Vladimir tried to remember each one of his past 19 lives. In the beginning of his first life, Vladimir was born into a family of farmers at some point during the 1800's. Like a dream that's been tucked away into the cover of a hidden drawer, memories of his first life were a wisp of smoky haze. A sudden rush of pain overrides the recollections taking place. Dabbing at the two drops of blood arising from the gash he had accidentally given himself, Vladimir caught a pleasant image of his parents.

Vladimir's mother was taller than her husband, square jawed and with a dancer's posture, Samantha Fortune dotted on her son Vladimir the way strict mothers from the old country did. Though she herself never revealed what country that may be, her past before meeting Clyde Fortune, Vlad's dad, are forever masked in the spin that surrounded her existence.

Clyde wasn't a mysterious man. Having inherited millions from his grandfather Riley Fortune, Clyde was left the remarkable responsibility of running or selling the family software company. He chose to sell and bought a gigantic mansion where he took to browsing over google searches. When Vladimir was born, Clyde finally had the son he so felt he was cheated out of.

"Vlad's father had went and become a faggot," Clyde would say to his grandson as they sat together in front of the fireplace. Clyde had taken it upon himself to instruct the heir to his throne. Forever drunk on whiskey, at his death, Vladimir's father mourned the loss of a father he had never known. Once the grandson inherited the empire, jealously ran deeper than bone morrow and Vlad's father took to the heinous act of murdering his only son. The second life wasn't nearly as bad.

Given the opportunity to live until 60 was a gift Vlad would only get once. It was in that second life that he truly knew peace, which in the grand scheme of things was the worst joke ever. Better to not have the knowledge of hope's existence, for ponder of its absence will steer one toward insanity.

◆

A knock at the bathroom door shattered the reminiscence our star had dove in. Clean shaven, yet still not recognizing his own face, he stared at eyes looking back like daggers.

"What do you want?" Vlad yelled through the door.

"Just making sure you don't need anything," Niki Brown's trembling voice responded.

"I'm fine, thank you," he said cutting short the anger building deep down in his belly. Not here, not now, calm and collected. Vladimir got ahold of himself.

"Ok, we'll be downstairs waiting."

"Waiting for what?"

"We said we were going to get dinner after you showered and shaved."

"Do you think we can just order in?"

"Sure, of course. That'd be no problem, Vlad."

"Thank you, Niki," Vlad said feeling guilt and regret creep in him. "I'm sorry," he started, "it's just a lot to take in all at once. Right now, this is the safest place for me. I think I'm going to stay in here for a little bit longer too."

The silence that cut through the space between the door to the bathroom and the hallway where Niki stood left a trail of blood seeping from comforts stomach.

"We understand," she finally said. "Take your time, we'll be downstairs."

Vlad stood motionless listening to the footsteps of his cousin drift away. He never understood why she had a habit of wearing six inch heels. Vladimir realized the faucet had been running for all of that time. He quickly turned the cold water off and shook his head. It felt good to rest thumbs upon his temple and massage away the delusions that crept into his brain. The reel did not want to stop however. Life had ended anticlimactically in his second existence, much like getting hit by a bus, which can be exciting to some.

Life three was a topsy-turvy ride of pleasantry and tragedy. Given the circumstances of our story I'll brush past the other 17 lives and sum them all up by saying; Vladimir Fortune had experienced the gambit of infinity's wrath by the time he was released from Company 23's prison.

Company 23 is well known to many, it holds the most secure and revered incarceration complexes in all the 50 companies of America. Built in 2023, Company 23's prison, known as Real On Lox or ROX, was by far the greatest prison ever designed. It was in the ROX that Vladimir lost his 19th life.

Downstairs sipping on a second bottle of wine, Niki Brown and her cousin Alain Machado were frozen in fear. The wine had worn away some of the hysteria the two were feeding each other with. However, desperate times had called for a desperate measure.

"I haven't smoked weed in so long," Alain said scrunching up his face in disgust at the joint Niki pulled out of her fro.

"It'll be ok," Niki said putting the weed to her lips and sparking it up. A few drags later to get it going, she passed the joint to Alain who took it acceptingly and took one long professional hit. Niki watched as the joint burned away before her eyes. After Alain began to cross into the land of no return, Niki interjected reaching for her shit. Exhausted wasn't the word for what they both felt. The waiting never ceased and the sun had begun to set. When night began to sprinkle itself fully upon the cousins, a truth be told moment erupted from the leftovers of resentment locked outside of the mirrors surrounding the egos.

"What are we going to do about him?"

"We stick to the plan. The bosses say they will contact us, so we wait until then."

"How long do you think that might be, Niki?"

"48 hours more than likely. Who knows, maybe sooner? These types tend to wrap up business in a hurry."

"I hope you're right," Alain said feeling the butterflies eating away at his insides.

"It takes time to assimilate back into regular life."

"This isn't regular life."

"Be careful Alain, you of all people know the harsh penalty given to those speaking ill on the order of things."

"There is slander and then there is factually stating what's happening."

"You can form it however you please. You know as well as I that it won't matter to the tribunal. You're lucky that the actions you've taken thus far haven't pounced death upon you."

So they waited. And waited. And waited.

It took two full hours before Niki galloped her way upstairs to the bathroom. The sounds of running water and a locked door met her. After yelling for Alain and getting the door open with his set of keys. A shade of stupidity fell over Niki Brown, Vladimir Fortune had escaped.

There was no telling where he may be. The fear of failure tugged at her but Niki paid it no mind. Only the next step blared its siren into her face. Losing nothing that couldn't be picked back up, a plan to capture Vlad began to take shape in Niki's mind.

Vlad was running for his life. It had begun to rain just as he crawled through the bathroom window out to the drainpipe he had shimmied down his entire life. Growing up in Sector 4 meant that Sector 4 was all whom you interacted with. Each company has about 20-24 Sectors. Sector 4 of company 23 wasn't a bad hood to live in at all.

◆ ◆ ◆

The outside air felt good upon Vladimir's face. Switching between all out sprinting and a light jog, Vlad kept moving. With no destination in mind there was no goal other than to continue to be free. Being in jail for ten years wasn't something he ever wanted to repeat again. Even if some of those years were spent in his last life.

It was a man whom introduced Vladimir Fortune to the conundrum that was his existence. Bouncing happily between lives, Vlad began to assume his experiences and more importantly the remembrances of his previous lives, were a cross between normal and out of the ordinary. When one life would cease, Vlad would die just as we all do. He would then be born into a new body with a new family and an entirely new life. It was the memories that would remain. How and why were questions Vladimir had yet to answer at the time of his release from prison and at that point he himself had given up all hope of ever knowing.

The man to introduce him to the plight of his semi-immortality was Mr. Chase, the piano player.

"Now, first of all," Mr. Chase began. He seldom did not have a cigarette dangling from his bottom lip. Always lit and ash hanging on by some invisible adhesive that awaited the enviable flick from Mr.

Chase into the ashtray that seemed to never be too far away. "Don't waste too much time wondering about how this is happening, it is, get over it. Time is a commodity we have more of for some strange reason. However, we still are slaves to it. Just slaves with a bit more room to stretch our legs."

"Are there others like us?" Vladimir asked as thought provoking questions furiously flashed through the lens of his mind.

"To my knowledge, I have only known five others like us, you being the fifth. The farthest I've ever seen one of us go is twenty lives. I know this because I myself am on my twentieth life."

"How do you know that 20 is the end of lives for you?"

"I can feel it young man, I can feel it deeply in my bones. There's nothing more pronounced than the approaching wind of death. No, this is the end for me, possibly, it's as far as we all can go."

Mr. Chase had no idea one way or the other. There was no way he could follow someone else's transition into another life and be able to say how many lives they each had. Nor was it ever known how many actually exist around the globe and through the universe. An infinities worth of wonder waves delightful fruits in our faces using time as a beating drum to keep us dancing.

"Now, the most important thing that you must understand when it comes to this opportunity and responsibility is that either you are to push beyond the monotonies of daily living, and cross over into a blissful life where you get to countdown the seasons of mortality in a slow leisurely pace. Or, you can take the radical route and attempt to break the mold of humanity for better or for worse. The choice is yours."

In the very best of ways, the next morning, Mr. Chase died of a heart attack while on the toilet. A bland end to an unknown remarkable man I must add. How is such the case often enough to care less following each encounter. Throwing away all manner of sanity, Vladimir began to doubt whether his memories of the lives lived previously were even real. Losing sleep and eventually weight, Vlad wasted away in great worry.

Glowing brilliantly of Crime and Punishment, there wasn't much left as Vladimir died in petrified grief.

Born into his next life, I believe was the seventh, a plan began to take shape in his mind. As Vlad increased in age, learned his ABC's and times tables. He moved his way upward toward that great seat of higher learning being broken down by its own stubborn adherence to archaic traditions. Power was meticulously gained, nourished and cultivated into a global network of support. At the end of this life, with no heirs to call his own, Vlad created a company that would flourish well into the next hundred years. Holding the secret password to the company's vault and being the only one to know the location, a great reach was obtained to keep a fortune after death.

Running himself dry, Vladimir stopped dead in his tracks. Unable to move, he flashed back to leaving the prison until now, so much time had been wasted. He wasn't even in the right Company to reach the vault. Remembering Sifu Ping's teachings, Vladimir returned to his happy place.

♦ ◆ ♦

"Pour over your thoughts until the river always flows beside your mind. Watch them float away until there is no longer any sight of them. Look at the moon reflect in the shimmering waters. Stop thinking about your thoughts that are floating down the river, beyond the horizon. The clear water's constant flow is the reality, naturally flowing and balancing all experiences with those lost to the memories' disjointed projection."

"If we don't find him soon the Fables will come down and correct this situation and us, Nikki." Alain said frantically to his cousin.

"Yes, Alain, I know. Please, you have to relax. There's no reason to get so frantic."

"I'm not frantic, I'm being rational. You can't pretend that we're not fucked."

"Language my dear man. Please, do not lower yourself to the mud with those around us. Remember your place in the Inner Circle."

"Don't talk to me about the Inner Circle; I don't want to hear it."

"Niki, you can't sit around and pretend like they don't own the very water we drink."

"Alain, you are far too frightful for your age. Why do you live to fear with what you believe will happen? Instead, live in the now, open doors and make opportunities happen in your life. I don't really think it will matter much in the grand scheme of things."

"That's the most encouraging thing I've heard all year, Nikki, thank you," Alain said sarcastically. "If you're finished critiquing me, I'd like to get back to the problem that's in dire need of a solution. What are we going to do about Vladimir Fortune?"

"My dear cousin. We know exactly where he is heading, now don't we?"

Alain Machado searched his brain ravenously opening filing drawers filled with dust.

"I hate that pitiful look that gets smacked across your face when you can't remember something. Reminds me of a lost dog or something. Focus, my dear Alain, focus I say. Think back to Thanksgiving, when we got our first break in the case against this man, Fortune."

"Ah, yes, before you had let him inside of you."

A dagger had been thrown, and it was Alain that drew first blood. The rivalry that had gone on since they were children, continued.

"My dear, Alain, do you really believe tha…."

"Stop calling me dear Alain, I can't stand it."

"My, my, look at you all fire and grit. Fright and folly. A man's man, are you? Do you want to hit me? Smack me in my face."

This last one seemed like an invitation to Alain, he had smacked his cousin before. To him, he didn't see her as a woman. Alain looked at Nikki as an equal whom stood worthy of his back hand. Smack her he did and it wasn't the first time she kicked his ass for doing so either.

SMACK!

The crescendo affect sent an echo of judgement racing through the silence that erupted throughout the COFFEE JOINT. Nikki Brown and her cousin, Alain Machado, were regulars in the espresso and tea establishment at the time of this outburst.

"I can't believe you hit me."

"You said to do it."

"I didn't think you would."

"Well, now you know not to offer up chances to things you're not willing to bet on."

"You bastard."

"Oh toughen up, lady. Or did you forget we still have a recently released domestic terrorist on the loose? Our only job. Our only task was to secure the mark and wait for pick-up. And because of your unprofessionalism, we couldn't' even do that."

"Now wait just a goddamn minute. Who are you calling unprofessional? I follow every guideline to the fucking T."

"All except the ones that entail a fucking domestic terrorist. I'm personally wondering how you were given the lead on this assignment. Given your track record, excuse my assuming. You at least blew the commanding officer, right. What's his name, Bryant?"

"Commander Bryant has a great family and an excellent wife."

"Funny how you separated the two. Seems to me through my recollection that a wife would constitute a family. Never separate are they, for the very beginnings they are to that great organization nature taps so many undeserving with." Digressions alone could not stifle the audacity of Nikki towards her cousin.

"Insulations are almost as deadly as assumptions. The past hasn't yet caught up to you. That much is clear. Though before all the audience members leave from boredom at the words sweeping across this page, I shall tell you a story. It is about a witch lost in a time where seldom little is cared for. One less haggard woman to deal with is what the patrons both said and agreed with as they themselves allowed a small minority take away their wealth until the land was only tar. This woman, who the town foolishly marked as a witch, neither was nor had ever professed any desire to be one. Yet, burned at the stake was she."

"Please don't sit here and try to distract me with one of your 'stories.' I've about had it with anything you have to say. To be perfectly honest, I have grown great shame at the very thought of being your friend."

Like an old married couple, the two argued pitting brooms against shoes in the fight for household dominance. Until one of them eventually gave. In this telling, it was losing the domestic terrorist Vladimir Fortune that provided Alain the extra narrative to dig into Nikki.

"Melt much butter, recently."

This joke worked against Nikki Brown, because her body was the one thing that mattered most to her.

"So tell me, Nikki. What have your people been telling you about me? Excuse me," Alain interrupted himself to answer his smart phone. "Do we know if the shipments all arrived on time?"

Nikki checked her smart phone. "All shipments will be notified once they arrive. Estimated time of arrival, approximately four days from today."

Niki checked her watch. It was December 1st. Where our memories lie, is where the great moment of writing for words thrives. So they both tried their hand at throwing their clad tones.

"Can we find this guy?" Alain asked his cousin, Nikki, waking her from napping.

"Yes, we can find him."

"I meant right now. Dangers lurk all around. What should I be on the lookout for?"

"Because you're needed."

"No, this is getting away from me."

"You really should just rest. I'm almost certain it will make you feel better."

"By taking a nap, that's your goddamn advice?

The presiding case ended in nothing other than banter and confusion. Lasting longer than what would be thrown from a balcony, a great tantrums worth of emotions spewed out. Contaminating the radio waves of brains in the vicinity, thunderous glamor erupted onto the great namesake which greets this stories protagonist. Returning to our current scene, a never before seen embarkation took place. Lowering the gates of hell, a remarkable thing never before was mentioned until now. In fact, 'tis the very situation before us, unfolding as it were, that makes the first of seven links connecting the structure of this a great tale.

◆ ◆ ◆

The concept of companies buying up countries was inevitable after the "bitcoin scam" that wiped out internet money as a viable currency. We should have seen it coming, of course. By the end of 2018 the fall of the great democratic empire was in full swing. America felt the hit hardest of all.

Nestled tightly inside of the place Vladimir discovered inside of himself while under the cruel tutelage of Sifu Ping, a memory jumped into his brain. It was that of the great ballerina Suzy Lee. Their acquaintance took place when Vlad was 17, in one of his previous 19 lives. He couldn't remember which, however. Vlad's father in this life was a Sergeant in the Army and the family was among those that scatter the globe so frequently. As an officer, Vlad's father instilled a greatness in the desire to serve. Duty and honor were etched into Vladimir's brain. Each life had brought to him more than ever was to be wished for; experience and wisdom were Vlad's wealth.

This meant nothing at the moment, however. The sun was setting and Vlad knew very soon that if he were caught on the street it would be disastrous. There was no doubt that the two would be calling in to report very soon. The pull of the memory was greater than Vlad had realized, upon first viewing. A forced revisit prompted the extension of stay in his happy place.

Suzy Lee made her enigmatic entrance through the introduction of a high school friend whom Vlad had made while attending the international school in China. During Vlad's senior year his dad was stationed in Ningbo. There was a great wave of experience brushed upon him and before long, along with his previous lives; a great weight that had been forming for some time began to crash down upon his shoulders.

Pushing such heavy challenges forces the body to push beyond its limits, which unfurls transformative results. Yet, the fact of violently tearing and breaking still remains. Recovery was always the most important factor in maintaining such strain.

"You should meet her," Vlad's friend Charlie said in Mandarin.

"I don't have time for any new friends right now," Vlad responded in Mandarin. Trying his best to skirt the subject, collecting his books into the bag he was carrying and prepared to leave.

"Now, wait just a moment," Charlie said standing and blocking Vladimir's path to exit. "Just hear me out." Charlie's Mandarin was naturally impeccable given that he himself was not only Chinese, but also a citizen of the great city of Ningbo. Charlie was in Vlad's class and their family homes were separated by a block. It was great luck connecting to a decent chum as soon as he landed in China. Charlie did a wonderful job helping Vlad get his sea legs, so to speak.

Out of respect for his friend, Vladimir Fortune sat back down on the bleachers of the school playground and prepared to listen.

"Now, her name is Suzy Lee. She's a ballerina."

Vlad rolled his eyes.

"Come on man. Why you so cynical about all this?"

"I'm not. I've just got a lot of work to do man. There's really nothing left for me to do but work every hour that I'm awake, if I'm to graduate."

"I keep telling you not to worry about this, man. They aren't going to fail you. You're the only foreigner in our entire school and there aren't that many in this entire province even. You're able to speak Chinese to me, I can understand you. You're not going to fail and that's the bottom line. You really will like this woman, Vlad. I'm telling you. You really should listen to me."

"Fine, I'll listen to you. Just go ahead and finish."

"Like I was saying….she's a ballerina, and a good one at that. Suzy was born into the famous Lee-Oswald family."

"The trust fund kids?"

"Exactly. Suzy is the granddaughter of one of the kids."

"Interesting."

"It gets even more interesting. She showed promise in ballet at the age of three and was therefore enrolled in the very best program the Lee-Oswald family could find. Fast forward 15 years later and we have Suzy Lee, gearing up for her starring performance in the Nutcracker Suite."

"I love the Nutcracker Suite. My parents used to take me to it every year for a period of time when I was six or nine, maybe."

"Wait until you see Suzy Lee in it."

"Is she that wonderful?" Vlad asked with excitement clearly visible in his face and could be heard even in his voice.

"Well, I myself haven't gotten to see her yet. The reviews have been marvelous though. She has been all throughout Europe, America and Japan. We're on her last stops of the tour. China gets one show and we got tickets," Charlie said as he pulled out two tickets.

Vlad can't believe his eyes and wonders if this is all a dream. Everything just seemed too scripted. Finding no harm in letting it play on just a bit longer, Vladimir allowed himself to float a bit farther into the mysteries held securely within the future.

"When is the show," is all he could muster to say.

"Tonight, of course," Charlie responded. A look snuck onto his face that vanished just as quickly. The look was a question of doubt arisen at Vlad's own insecurity.

"I can't do tonight."

"Whatever your plans are, just change them man. I'm offering you a chance at meeting your future wife. Right here, right now. Break your appointment."

"It's an appointment that I just cannot break."

"Ok, I hear ya...but can you really not break this appointment? Are you yourself going to save someone, because your hands are the special hands that can save a person's life? 'Cause if not, then you're just wasting my time."

"That doesn't seem like a good way of convincing me to break my appointment. I don't even know what this Sandra Lee looks like."

"Suzy Lee," Charlie corrected, beginning to show exasperation for his friend Vladimir.

"Excuse me. I remembered the Lee." A silence fell upon the two friends and then Vlad remembered what it was he was going to say. "You expect me to go out there on my own with no picture or background to back up your claim that this woman is the exceptional beauty I am missing from my life?"

"That is exactly what I expect you to do."

"I'm not sure that I can do that, Charlie."

"Well then at least go out of obligation, since I bought a ticket for you, my friend."

"Well played. Sure, I'll go. What time does it start at?"

"5pm."

"That only leaves us 45 minutes. Charlie, what the hell man?"

"Don't worry, everything's been arranged."

With these words leaving Charlies mouth, a black Mercedes limousine pulled up to the entrance of the school. Charlie had been directing Vladimir who was already in a rush to get home. Before being trapped into the ticket guilt trip, Vlad knew they were expensive tickets. Besides, he really did like the Nutcracker very much. The aroma, the costumes, the dances, everything. The entire production was one Vlad had always approved of. The night could only be fun. For this reason alone there was no reason to gripe or complain, so along they went.

◆ ◆ ◆

Once settled into their seats and swimming in that wonderful awe inspiring moment just before the show begins, the silence that befalls the audience can be heard and the atmosphere changes as the orchestra begins with the curtains going up.

Vlad hummed and nodded along as he had done at the first production he had seen. It was a strange thing to have never seen the Nutcracker after having lived so many lives. But once he had, every life thereafter, a great portion was spent in petrified glee at the story. It was truly a treat to see the productions evolve as each generation progressed. Observing a small portion of infinity for a brief moment forced Vlad to appreciate the nuances of history more so than others.

As the Sugar Plum Fairy played and the dancers danced, Vladimir was transfixed at the image before him of Suzy Lee twirling elegantly in and out of his heart. Charlie was right, he was in love.

Suzy Lee had endured and sacrificed beyond what would ever be written about. Her source of drive was a mystery as she performed in Shanghai for her future husband and the packed audience. A feeling of reaching out overcame her, almost causing her to stumble in a pivotal portion of the show. Recovering like the professional she was, Suzy went on to finish the performance to rave reviews, however, I never read them.

"Are you sure this is going to be ok?"

"Don't worry, I told you. We go way back. She's going to just melt all over you. It's a good thing you can speak Chinese though. She don't know no English."

"Yea, good thing," Vlad said laughing nervously.

"Relax man. This is going to be great."

A few knocks later and the door opened, it was a giant door made of oak. The door itself looked like the trunk of a tree, it was that large. Vladimir stood before Suzy Lee in overalls and a yellow long sleeved shirt underneath. A smile extending to beyond greeted Vlad; Suzy was very excited to meet him.

"I really enjoyed your performance," Vlad said to Suzy after the two of them had gotten settled and Charlie made his smooth exit. There wasn't much room in the tiny bathroom that had been reconstructed into a make-up booth. Suzy pulled out a bottle of Jack Daniels and they made do.

"I'm glad you drink," she said to Vlad.

"Why is that?"

"It's easier to talk to people that drink. People that don't drink tend to be too serious. The most serious are those that drink but for health reasons or another, must steer clear. I think that's the worst. I don't mind quitting a thing. What pisses me off are the forces that demand you to quit, Death ultimately is the only pronounced threat thrown at us day-to-day."

"I'm not so sure I can agree on that. I've met a lot of people that are absolutely great conversationalist and are stone cold sober. I think it just depends on the person."

"I don't. They are doing a great job of hiding it. There is anger and hate tucked away on an island somewhere collecting dust. All it takes is that one helicopter to save that anger and hate just sitting there, waiting for that opportune moment to strike."

"You certainly are a bundle of sunshine, aren't you?"

"Am I scaring you, Vladimir?"

"Suzy, I want you to look into my eyes. What do you see?"

"I see two eyes looking back at me."

"And those eyes, what do you think they are hiding behind in that cave where thoughts flow by like Spring Rivers?"

"There's a lot behind those eyes," Suzy said inching closer to Vladimir. Unconsciously, they moved to kiss and embrace.

"I've fallen into your eyes," Suzy Lee said the next morning while she and Vlad were in bed.

"That's alright," he responded not understanding the implications of what she was trying to get at.

◆ ◆ ◆

A sharp cackle of thunder broke Vladimir's reverie. In a matter of moments following the heavens clapping, rain began to cascade down upon Vlad. Drenching him quickly, Vlad fled the street he had been wandering and sought shelter from the rain. A small mom and pop grocery called Gino's provided an awning to hide underneath. Vlad peered into the glass window to see if the establishment was open. It was. A ring of the bell above the front door startled the old man at the cash register. He gathered himself and focused his gaze on our star, Vladimir Fortune.

Young and strong with an elongated posture proper as a dancers, Vlad walked forward to the owner of the grocery. His gait was labored from running most of the day.

"How can I help you, son?" Gino asked in greeting Vlad.

"Do you have anything to drink?"

"Water is in Aisle 3," he said, raising an eyebrow in suspicion.

"Thank you."

Stumbling his way through the grocery shelves, Vlad found the section filled with water. Snatching a gallon off the shelf the water bottle in his hand pulled his center of gravity to the right. A lean to which pulled pain at his side. Aside from that, everything was just dandy. Gino begged to differ, however.

"How much will that be?" Vlad asked tossing the gallon water bottle onto the sales counter.

Gino eyed the water bottle before raising his gaze slowly to look fully upon Vladimir. He shook his head at the state of the young man before him.

"I don't need your pity, old man," Vlad said surprised at what came forth from his lips. "Just tell me how much this is and I'll be on my merry way."

"For you, $30.00."

"$30.00!?"

"Yes, very good deal for you. On sale from $50.00."

"I thought it was only $15.00," Vlad said genuinely shocked. Forgetting he had been in prison the last ten years.

"Young man, didn't you hear that water went up $10.00 last week. Where've you been?"

Vladimir scoffed to himself. "Prison, I've been in prison."

"Oh," the old man Gino said with solemn eyes. "Well, yes. Things have been pretty bad for Company 23. All the companies really. The President doesn't give a rat's ass about us. There's nothing that can be done. Pretty soon, most folks won't be able to afford water. What happens then? Most believe they'll just let us die."

"Let's hope it doesn't come to that," Vlad said shuffling in his pockets for the little notes he had left. "I'm sorry, I only have $20.00."

"I'll give it to you for $15.00. Seeing as how you just got out, I know you probably need a little bit of support. Not many left in this country, but decent folk do still exist."

"I should say you are a king among the most decent."

"That's very kind of you to say, thank you."

Vladimir paid the old man Gino and collected his gallon water bottle.

"Do you mind if I hang out in your grocery store for a while. I haven't any place to go at this particular moment," Vlad asked the innocence of himself flashing out.

Gino looked upon the young gentleman with sorrow in his heart.

"Yes, of course. You can stay as long as you like. I'm going to be closing up in about 45 minutes. You're welcome to stay afterwards but I would ask that you help me close up. I was thinking of ordering a vegan pizza and watching an old Orson Welles picture."

"Which film?" Vlad asked interested. In his 17th life he was married to a man that was an Orson Welles fanatic. Those times were as grand as the first 5 lives he remembered living. A' last, there wasn't a moon of hope left in him after the 19th life, all feeling was taken from Vladimir's heart.

After devouring most of the pizza, the credits began to roll in the movie, and the old owner of the grocery began to tidy up.

"I couldn't imagine being tossed into such a predicament," Vladimir said as he gathered up the trash into the large Bounty bag Gino had handed him.

"What predicament is that?" Gino asked.

"Being married to a Nazi."

"You'd be surprised what people often find themselves in, young man. I am sure you yourself were never expecting to spend time in jail."

"Pops, my time in jail was nothing compared to the time that I've done over the last few lifetimes."

"Whatever do you mean," Gino asked stopping from his task of cleaning up the section of the grocery they had been enjoying.

For just a second, Vlad thought of telling the old man exactly what he meant. As the conversation played out in his mind, however, Vladimir thought better of it.

"I don't mean anything really. Must just be the wine talking. This is my first drink in a decade, after all."

"I did some time myself back in the day."

"Did you now, old man?"

"Not as much as you, and this was a very long time ago…when I was younger."

"Time is time though."

"I suppose that is true. Anyway, I'm certain you had some hooch inside as much as I did. Even all those years ago, I'm sure not that much has changed."

Vladimir laughed in pleasant agreement. "You got me there old man. I did have my share of hooch. It didn't take the other inmates long to initiate me to their wonderful drink."

"Judging by the looks of you, you must've been pretty young when you went in."

"Yes, I was awfully young," Vlad responded as the dark cloud of remorse fell over his eyes as flashbacks of life in the cell he called home for ten years passed through his mind.

"Well, I've got to head home to my wife. I'm afraid you'll have to be leaving now, son."

"Yes, of course. Thank you so much for the water, old man."

"You're welcome, young man," Gino said. Vlad turned his back to the sales counter and made to leave. The image of the destitute young man creeping away toward what could only be his death once he stepped under the clouds unnerved the grocery store owner. "Say, do you have a place to sleep?" he asked.

Vlad turned and looked his sunken eyes into Gino's own.

"No idea, sir," he responded.

"That's no good," Gino responded shaking his head. "Tell you what. I'll phone up The Father and ask him to let you sleep at the church tonight. He'll probably have you do a few chores, but that's a fair trade for a safe place to sleep and a hot meal to eat."

"Yes, thank you. That's awfully generous of you. I happen to be Buddhist, though. I'm not sure how that will take."

"It'll be just fine. You don't know The Father; he's the most honest man in this neighborhood. I'll call him now. Trust me, it'll be all good."

Vladimir didn't have very much effort left in him to put up a fight. He had fled on impulse, without thought or plan. There wasn't any logic to the crime he was committing of fleeing his handlers. Vlad was lucky even to have two of his friends assigned to the job. So he went along with the old man's idea and allowed himself to be whisked away to the church just up the block from the grocery store.

Father Clementine was an even older man than Gino the grocer. The wrinkles in his skin told a story of great sacrifice and a faith that was unbreakable. The nobility of physical weakness burst forth strength in the face of adversity. Father Clementine had shed his share of sweat and blood to protect the church Vladimir Fortune had just walked into.

The Father wasn't a preachy priest nor was he very talkative. I dare say that was his appeal and why for the last sixty years he has been the head of the Church. As far as Father Clementine was concerned, the great stone sanctuary was his castle to protect at all cost. A refuge for many at times of turmoil and chaos, disaster seems to have visited every possibility of a life worth living. Father Clementine could feel the heavy weight burdening Vladimir as he shuffled forward in tow behind Gino.

"It's good to see you, Mr. Hopper. How is the family?"

"It's good to be seen, Father. The family's doing pretty well. How've the days been treating you?"

"Oh you know…nothing to complain of for me. My hands stay full providing hope to those that wish for it."

"Well, I've brought you a young man that is in dire need of provisions."

"I must say, you do attract all types of people don't you, Mr. Hopper?"

"What can I say? I got a knack for pulling those that need help to me. Seems it's my duty to help em'. Just trying my best here."

"I think you're doing a fine job. Wouldn't you agree?" Father Clementine asked Vlad, acknowledging him for the first time. Vlad shook as a cold chill enveloped his body. Goose pimples arose over his exposed skin. Breathing rapidly, clouds of breath formed from Vlad's lips. Something has just entered the church, Father Clementine thought to himself, noticing Vlad's acute awareness to the change.

This boy is much older than his age allows for, The Father continued to think while eyeing Vladimir carefully. Whatever just entered the church is here because of the boy.

"Father," Gino said breaking the Priest from his thoughts.

"Yes, Mr. Hopper."

"I best be going now. My wife'll think I'm at the bar drinking if I don't come home right away after closing up the store."

"Yes, of course. Please, get home swiftly. Tell Laura I said hello."

"I sure will Father. You should turn the heat up in here, its freezing," Gino said grabbing his arms and hugging himself as he walked to exit the church.

Vladimir and Father Clementine both stood, staring off into their own space, as the large front door of the church creaked open and then slammed shut. The echo reverberated around the religious chamber. The chill left and the temperature began to return to normal.

"Are you hungry, son?" Father Clementine asked breaking the silence.

Vlad felt his stomach sucking in. As if responding itself to Father Clementine's question, Vlad's stomach began to growl painfully, bringing him to his knees.

"I'll take that as a yes," Father Clementine said laughing to himself. He departed leaving Vlad on the floor of the church. Gathering up some items from the kitchen, the Father returned with a basket of fruit, bread, nuts and raisins. And, last but not least, a large half empty bottle of brandy. He helped Vladimir to his feet and had to half-carry him to the kitchen area where there was a table and chairs for the Priests to take their meals.

Vladimir slumped down with a thud into the metal folding chair. His stomach let out another painful groan.

"You're going to have to take your time and eat slowly. Sounds like you haven't had anything to eat in quite some time."

The words were coming in clear but there was no sense to be made of them. Vlad's heartbeat overpowered everything eventually and a great sheet of blackness came down over all the existence that was the moment.

◆ ◆ ◆

Remembering past lives seems like it would be a good thing. To experience generation after generation in a fresh new way; being able to learn things quicker because they were already maintained in the previous life. For Vladimir Fortune, it just wasn't like this.

Sure, he could remember just as well as most adults can remember childhood. But like all memories, his was unreliable as your very own. No, the torment of Vladimir Fortune is that he could never stop regretting the mistakes made in every life. Regrets arise in human life as the moon reflects at night in the river. A sumptuous sway catches the gaze as the scent of an unknown prey marches toward its very own grave.

These were the songs that played in Vladimir's brain as he came to. Father Clementine was standing over him, patting at his forehead with a wet towel. Vladimir began to study the man's wrinkled face and could feel the stories each crease shared.

"You're alright, son?"

"Would you please stop calling me son? I had a bastard of a father once that called me 'son.' I eventually hit him over the head with a hammer. I'd rather not have to do that to you, Father."

Taken aback, Father Clementine recoiled from the increasingly more dangerous man he had agreed to take in. A torrent of rage could be felt building from within Vladimir. Both were shocked at the vast amount that could be felt. The cold chill returned. Father Clementine knew what was happening.

"My apologies, young man. What shall I call you?"

"Vladimir is fine."

"It is, indeed. Tell me, would you like to drink some brandy and eat some bread? I should say that'll be just what you need to awaken yourself."

"Ain't no purpose. I'm screwed anyway." Vladimir tried to raise himself but quickly fell back down upon the church kitchen floor.

"You best stay down there for the time being. I'd say we can just set up a little picnic type of setting and have our meal down here, on the floor."

"That doesn't seem very sanitary, Father."

"I think we'll be ok. The boys clean this kitchen three times a week. Between them and those cleaning it for punishment, I'd say this kitchen gets cleaned almost daily. Now, how about that brandy? A little brandy in the belly always does the trick. Just a little though, not a lot."

"I can't argue against a drink," Vlad said leaning his back against a floor cabinet near the sink. Settling himself in a spot that was comfortable and to his liking, Vlad started to feel himself giving up.

"What should we cheers to?" Father Clementine asked Vlad after getting a filled glass into each of their hands.

"There's nothing worth cheering to father."

"Look, Vladimir, if you're going to drink with me then you must drop this awfully morbid talk. Melancholy ain't no place for drinking."

"I'm sorry, Father. You just couldn't understand how bleak my world is."

"You'd be surprised to know, Vladimir that you aren't the only person that's suffering."

"Oh father I know that. You don't understand. I've been suffering 19 times over. Entire lives. I've lived them. The highs, the lows, I remember it all and it's driving me crazy."

"Slow down now, Vladimir. Let's drink. Toast to friendship."

The word shot a sharp bolt into Vlad's psyche, penetrating him to the core for a brief moment, clarity entering his brain. How many friends had Vlad known? How many had he loved? How many betrayed him? Countless friends, even still a handful matter. Even less than those, two stand out above all others. Moving hazy pictures with antiquity projected their images between a dream and memories. Sydney and Ralph were great friends from two different lives. Sydney was from the life where he was just released from prison. Ralph was from his fourth life.

Sydney was a friend from the last childhood Vlad would possibly ever have.

The clank of the glasses filled with brandy dissolved the images of Vladimir's two friends away from his mind's eye. A drink sounded nice right about now to Vladimir. As the liquid sloshed into his belly warming his esophagus on the way down, Vladimir struck a chord in his life condition that brought him back to a calm he hadn't experienced since being released from prison earlier that morning.

"You enjoyed the brandy, huh?" Father Clementine said after Vlad swallowed the last drop in the glass he was holding.

"I did," he answered holding out the empty glass to be refilled.

Father Clementine did just that. "It's rather odd for a man of your youth to know the enjoyments of a good brandy. Did this father you speak of that was such a bastard drink his share of brandy? Perhaps that's why he was such a bastard. Too much brandy can do that to a man, tends to often be the story."

"That father didn't drink. He was just a bastard naturally. I did have a father from the first lives that enjoyed a good brandy. He would let me have a sip with him by the fireplace every Thursday night. This was before they started making a big deal about letting children drink."

"I don't think I understand. How were you living at this time?"

"It's a bit of a long story Father. From the looks of that bottle, you don't seem to have enough brandy for its telling."

"My dear Vladimir, for a good tale there is always enough brandy. I suggest you get some food in you though before you go off on any long soliloquies. Please, enjoy to your hearts content. Do be slow about it though. I'll go and fetch a few more bottles of brandy so that we can enjoy this story of these many lives you seem to have lived."

Father Clementine disappeared down into the cellar, leaving Vladimir to stare at the basket before him, filled to the brim with food. Much like a scared cat, he crept his way toward the basket and picked out cautiously pieces of bread. It wasn't long, however, before Vlad took caution of the wind and dug in. When Father Clementine returned with bottles in his hands and under his arms, Vlad was once again clutching his stomach in pain.

"I told you not to eat too fast," the Father said scolding Vladimir. "Let's get you into the wash closet."

"Why are you being so kind to me?" Vladimir asked after he had emptied his stomach into the toilet bowl and was lowered onto a cot Father Clementine gathered from the closet.

"It's my duty to help those in need, especially young men such as ye carrying around the burdens of the world."

"I'd have to agree with you on that one, Father. My burden is that I can never die and rest easily."

"Give it time, Vladimir. You've got plenty of years ahead of you to alter the direction of your fate. Death for you has the possibilities of being met by the heavenly judgment of acceptance."

"Father, no disrespect but I've died many times. All you do is come back. It's like being asleep and having a nice pleasant dream. And then waking in a brand new body that you have to wait to grow and develop and learn so many important things to be human in. Over and over again I've done this. I don't even know when it will end. Hopefully this is the last one. But then at the same time, if this is the last out of all twenty of the lives I've lived, this one is the most important of them all. And ten years of the most precious life I've ever lived I've already spent in prison."

"I'm afraid I don't follow you, Vladimir."

"There's not really much to explain, Father. I've died 19 times and have been re-born 20."

"I see. And you can remember all of your past lives."

"That's correct."

"And 20 is as far back as you can remember?"

"I suppose there could be more, but for the most part it's as far back as I can remember."

"What is the farthest back in time you can remember, if you don't mind me asking out of curiosity?"

"The earliest date that pops into my head is somewhere around the year 1312."

"You'll understand if I find this incredibly hard to believe."

"How do you think I feel? I was prosecuted and coerced into a facility, at the end of one of my lives by my wife and her sisters."

"How unfortunate."

"Yes. I spent the last 15 years of that life locked in an asylum. A fire one of the patients started eventually took me out while I slept."

"You remember this?"

"That? No actually I don't. I came across a headline some lives later talking about the hospital burning down and found my name. I have a list of 19 names, Father. Many of which have aliases. In over half of my lives I lived the lives of two men, at the very least in each life."

"It's so confusing. How've you been able to keep track of it all?"

"That's the problem, Father. I can't, I'm all mixed up. I don't know what's real and remembered or made up. What's daydreamed or dreamed and from which life. At this point I'm not even sure if I know what reality even means anymore."

"Vladimir, you've got to cherish the moments. That's all that needs to be a concerned worry."

"Hakunamatata, Father. Ain't no passing phrase."

"It means no worries," Father Clementine began to softly sing.

"For the rest of your days," Vlad joined him.

"It's our problem free," they sang in unison. Rising slowly in vibrato. "Phil-o-sophy. Hakunamatata."

After a few more songs aided by more brandy, Father Clementine and Vladimir had bonded nicely.

The next morning, or early afternoon, Vladimir stepped forth from the church that had been his refuge. Bidding farewell to Father Clementine, Vlad set out to see about conquering another day.

"Why don't you try and look up some old friends?" the Father suggested as parting last words of advice for the young Vladimir Fortune. "You've been away for so long. I'm sure no matter how you left them, they'll be happy to see you.

The faces of Sydney and Ralph again flashed in Vlad's mirror. The inner narrator that's never seemed to cease over 19 lives, still persisted in the 20th. Looking the Father in the eye Vladimir felt that about all he could do was keep such a request from the old man to heart and give it a good try. There happened to be an inclination creeping its way into the heart of Vlad that Sydney would be easy to find.

"I'll see what I can do about it," Vlad said waving goodbye and heading out on the street. Why did he think he could find Sydney? It didn't make any sense. Vlad wasn't much of a religious person. In the 20th life he was living he was born a Buddhist, so he always called himself a Buddhist. Vlad never cared much what circumstances he was born in as each life passed by. Each was a roll of the dice that Vlad would take his chance on. It was the later lives, especially the last two that the adventure turned into something of a nightmare.

Father Clementine stood outside the church entrance for some time, watching Vladimir walk away toward the horizon. When the dot that was the young man disappeared beyond the Father's line of sight, a vibration from the pocket of the robes he wore stirred against his thigh.

"You should be tracking him now," Father Clementine said into the Samsung smart phone. "No, he doesn't suspect a thing. To be honest, I'd say he's still imprisoned in his own mind. Locked into the tragically twisted fate the universe laid out upon him." Father Clementine started to realize he was beginning to feel sorry for the poor bastard. The moment, however, passed quickly. "The farthest back he can remember is 20 lives. Say, how many lives has this guy lived? Damn, really? That many, huh? Well, now I can understand the countries' interest in obtaining a sample to study and replicate. What was that? Oh yes, the Nano bots should be working havoc on his liver and kidneys momentarily. Remember, after 12 hours they'll patch up all they've eaten away and dissolved out of him. It only works if you get this injection into him, otherwise, you will have killed what could possibly be an immortal man."

# *Chapter Two:*
## An Unexpected Death and an Implant Leads to More

Jaqueline Brutus was Vladimir's wife; from which life he can barely remember. She was heir to the Brutus family fortune acquired through gold, railroads and bootlegging. Jaqueline Brutus was brought up to be a spoiled princess whom understood rarely the pleasantries of not being snooty. Her uncle was a regular Charles Foster Kane living on his own Xanadu. Vladimir would meet his future wife at her Uncle Tom's pleasure palace. Jaqueline was not one of the women on display, however, along with the men. Anything a millionaire desired was achieved on Tom Suarez's Worry Free Island.

The name was lousy and the operation illegal. Jaqueline's uncle was eventually busted for prostitution and possession with the intent to sell. It was international laws he was breaking too, so the world said bye to Tom Suarez. Worry Free Island was left to Vladimir's wife. She was ecstatic. Vlad was not at all. In this life, Vlad had taken to writing and with a great deal of difficulty was able to break through publishing a few bestsellers. Making enough to marry the heir of a tycoon, Vlad ended up setting himself up pretty well. He was crazy in love with Jaqueline and she was murderous for Vladimir. They were a match made in heaven. And then came the ownership of Worry Free Island.

The name alone caused Vladimir to detest the very idea of living upon such a fraudulent place.

"But my uncle left it to me," Jaqueline whined day after day as Vladimir packed and unpacked their things.

"I'm tired of this, Jaqueline. There can't be a single moment longer spent here."

"Why do you detest it so?" she asked with genuine shock in her voice. "You have everything you could ever dream, everything you could ever hope to achieve. All at your fingertips. You'd be a fool to walk away from such a life."

"Then I guess you married a fool, my dear. For I am departing company with you immediately." With that, Vlad walked right out of the house and marched his way toward the ferry preparing to depart for the day. Vlad marched away in the same manor he had left Father Clementine.

Back at the house he had fled, unbeknownst to Vlad, Niki Brown and Alain Machado watched on the GPS device. Between them the green dot represented Vladimir's position. The brandy Father Clementine had allowed Vlad to drink so freely from was infused with nano-bytes that attach themselves to the blood stream, sending a digital ping to whomever being tracked. Niki and Alain were tailing Vlad.

"Now we've got him," Niki said glaring at the green flashing dot.

"It's not good that he got involved," Alain said a fear rising in his voice that had not been there before.

"What're you so afraid of? The little old priest?"

"You don't know who these people are do you, Niki. These are not people that are to be toyed with."

"Who's playing games? I'm not, that's for sure. Vladimir Fortune is out there and needs be caught. Catching him will make my career. There can be no error when it comes to this. Do you understand me, Alain?" Niki's eyes burned with rage as she pierced Alain's gaze. As she drove the grey Volkswagen slowly through traffic, the small green blimp on the screen Alain held screamed out at her. Taunting her with the one shot she ever had gotten to climb her way out of the common life, 90% of all living in the 50 companies are destined for you to be shackled.

For Niki Brown the rage went deeper than any ulcer could burn, growing up without a desperation upon the hearts of great men and women. So true even more so for those of us that are ordinary and doubtful.

"Where's he heading now?" Niki snarled at her husband.

"Still heading straight. Seems like he's mobile at this moment."

"How did he get money for a car?"

How indeed. There wasn't anything tricky happening. Father Clementine had slipped Vladimir some money for a ride to see his friend, Sydney, and to get a warm meal or two depending upon how he spent his money. A taxi rolled by just in the nick of time. Hailing it to a halt, Vlad hopped in and directed the driver toward his destination.

The ride was a peace Vlad had not had the opportunity to enjoy for quite some time. Watching the section of company 23 he was passing by, a melancholy thoughtfulness overcame Vlad.

"How's your day going?" Vlad asked the driver trying to push away any chance of recollection and reflecting.

"Day's going pretty well," the man behind the wheel responded.

"You been working long?"

"Earlier, yea. Just got off a long beak though. You are my first customer as a matter of fact."

"I should find that lucky for me then."

"I guess that depends on how I drive."

"Please get us there in one piece."

"You've got nothing to worry about. This is the safest car you've ever been in. And when you step out, you'll see that you only take caution 'cause you'll maybe never be in a safer place again."

"I'll keep that in mind."

"You should do more than that. But to each man his own path."

The driver wove the taxi he commanded through traffic effortlessly in Captain Ahab fashion. Chasing not a white whale but merely the destination Vladimir told him to go, deeper into the woods our hero ventured.

Traffic. How much time had been wasted in traffic over all of our lives? How much time was spent thinking of all those things we've considered to be more than what we thought they could ever possibly be. Listening to the traffic noises—horns, tires on road, tires screeching and the outside life of Company 23—of what used to be California.

"I need to make a stop real quick," the driver said unexpectedly. "You don't mind, do you?"

Vladimir should've minded, but he knew he didn't.

"Yea, that's fine. I'm in no rush."

"Great. I appreciate that. I will comp your ride for being such a swell guy."

"You don't have to do that?"

"Sure I do. You can give a tip if you feel like you must do something."

That's pretty fair, Vladimir thought to himself. Smiling he asked the driver, "Where are you making a stop at?"

"The psychic," the driver said with a straight face.

"You're going to go see a psychic?" Vlad asked confusingly.

"No, my wife went to go see one. I need to pick her up."

"Oh, I see. That's nice. Is it far?"

"No, not far. Maybe twenty minutes. You sit back and relax. I'll play you some good music and give you this."

The driver handed Vladimir a black vape pen. Vlad took the pen and raised an eyebrow at the possible contents.

"It's good," the driver said watching Vlad through the rearview looking glass.

"I'll take your word for it."

The car pulled up to La Cienege. The driver flipped a 'U' and parked the passenger curbside. A very pregnant woman stood outside a small shop. 'Psychic' in neon lights illuminated the doorway. Velvet red carpet draping the floor bounced the highlighter low tone red bulbs sizzling around the psychic's work desk.

"Would you mind helping me?"

"Ok."

The psychic was an old short Polish woman with a multiple-packs-a-day husky voice. Her eyes were glossed over white and it seemed she could barely see through the cloudy film. She could see just fine, though. As Vladimir helped the driver's wife into the passenger's side, the psychic walked up to Vlad and tapped him on the shoulder.

The tap startled, Vlad. Turning around with caution, his body loosened when he saw the old woman's weathered face.

"Can I do anything for you, ma'am?" Vlad asked with a bow of acknowledgement.

"Young man, I would like to take a look at your palm."

"I'm not sure I really want to do anything at the moment."

Just then the driver's wife spoke up as the two gentlemen got her settled into the passenger seat. "I would listen to her if I were you. The fact that she approached you means something."

"What does it mean?" Vlad asked, the notion of alarm rising in his voice.

"I don't know. You've got to let her look at your palm to find out and see."

"You can go," the driver said as he fastened the safety belt across his wife's big belly. "It's the least I can do for your flexibility. She's so close to being due, I don't like to be too far away for too long. She's always moving around, making my heart go weak."

"You already comped me the ride. I don't want to take up anymore of your time."

"You gave him the ride for free?!" the driver's wife angrily exclaimed.

The driver rolled his eyes and gave me a look of thanks. "Just go, we'll be right here…now I've got to deal with this."

"Let me read your palm," the psychic said again. Her crooked smile shined a brilliant yellow that turned Vlad into butter. Taking his hand, the psychic lady pulled Vladimir into her office.

"Please, get settled. What hand do you write with?"

"Umm, my left."

"Great. Put it up on the table, palm up. That's good. Alright let me see. Hmm."

There was a silence. Very short, but worth mentioning.

"You're going to have a long life," she began reading Vladimir's palm. "You've got something coming to you. Something big. A battle I see on the horizon, for you. There seems to be a great many people looking for you. You've been running for a long time. Now, all of that comes to an end."

The psychic woman paused and looked at Vladimir's eyes. Turning toward the tissue box at her feet, she grabbed one and blew her nose.

"Excuse me," she said wiping her nose clean. "I'm not sick, it's just these damn allergies." The psychic woman took out a small bottle of sanitizer and spread some on her hands. "There, now I can touch you again. This is not so much as an end but a beginning. You think that time has run out for you. How wrong you will soon discover. I see, a woman will soon enter your life. An older woman. She will hold many keys to doors you must walk through. This woman will ferry you over to the next stage. It's all coming to a convergence, Vladimir."

Vlad couldn't recall whether or not he had told the woman his own name.

"That'll be all," the psychic woman said abruptly ending the palm reading session.

"Thank you," Vlad said standing perplexed as to what to do. "How much do I owe you?" he asked remembering his manners.

"No charge young man. You are on a quest and there was a spirit that seemed to want to give you a helping hand."

"How do I thank this spirit?"

"By staying true to the course. There will be many temptations. You must not waver. But you will, unfortunately I feel. Anyway, Godspeed to you on your journey. Tell Ishmael that his wife will deliver very soon."

"Ishmael?"

"The driver."

"Oh, ok sure. I'll tell him. Thank you again for everything. I appreciate the reading."

"It was my pleasure, Vladimir. Good luck."


Back in the car Vladimir Horowitz—our hero's namesake for the 19TH and 20th life he is living—is playing. Vlad's mother, Cyndy, was an avid fan of the great pianist. From the time that she was able to speak, which was incredibly young, Cyndy was moved to play the piano. On a whim chance, her instructor played Horowitz while they were on a break and Cyndy was captivated from that point onward. For that reason, Vlad could recognize almost any piece of Horowitz, so much had his mother played the grandiose pianist over the course of childhood for his 20th life.

It was the Polonaise in F Sharp Minor, Op. 44 playing that Vlad climbed into the car on. This version was by Frederik Chopin, another one of his mother's favorites. Obtaining and remembering multiple lifetimes worth of useful knowledge was one positive, considering Vlad's point of view.

After the first life was extinguished and forever lost to the memories of those living the first subsequent rebirth that Vlad remembered was filled with a vague familiarity. There's something that he soon discovered about having done things before in a past life. It creates almost a feeling of deja vu for him. For Vladimir deja vu is a force he has only felt on rare occasions, and one for which he is grateful to have occur in his last few lives.

The tracked changed over into Horowitz playing Hungarian Rhapsody No. 2. The twinkly keys sounding off playfully inside of the car engulfed Vlad in a feeling of pleasurable delight. The dun dun dun dunnn picks up and instantly, the memory of the movie "Who Framed Roger Rabbit" popped into his head. The scene when Eddie Valiant, who fights crime valiantly, is in the night club where Betty Boop is serving drinks, with her finely drawn figure moving across the screen. Daffy and Donald Duck are facing off in a piano contest. The crowd is lost in entertainment as the squid with a dozen arms serves drinks behind the bar and penguins dressed in snappy tuxedos walk around taking orders.

Vlad thought on the idea of cartoons walking amongst the augmented reality of humans and what the existence of a 'Cartoon World' where physics falls under the playful games of a Looney Tunes show looks like. Then the scene that comes next in 'Who Framed Roger Rabbit' burst its image onto Vlad's moving picture reel inside his brain. The voice of Jessica Rabbit seductively bellows out the blues anthem 'Why don't you do right' as horn dog men hoot and holla. Her extra voluptuously drawn motif, glittering in the sparkly red dress screamed obscenity.

"You had plenty money, 1922. You let other women make a fool of you. Why don't you do right, like some other men do? Get outta here, get me some money too," Jessica Rabbit sang prancing around the stage.

The track once again changed, breaking the scene in the movie from Vlad's memory. Another Horowitz, Piano Concerto No. 23 in A. Mozart was good to zone out to.

"So, where are we heading," Ishmael the driver finally asked as they pulled onto the highway.

"I need to go to Marina Del Rey."

"Ok, let me drop my wife off first and then I'll take you wherever you want to go."

"Sure," Vladimir responded. Complacency had washed over him. Exhausted, confused and with no plan; Vlad listened to the Horowitz hour on the classical station playing.

After helping Ishmael get his wife upstairs to their apartment and having an obligatory glass of lemonade made fresh by the woman due to immediate possible delivery at any moment, the two were back in the car.

"Ok. Marina Del Rey it is," Ishmael said as he knocked the car into gear and drove off.


Niki and Alain had been following the green blimp for the last few hours. Traffic was horrendous and they almost lost the Black Toyota Camry Sedan two times. Inside the car, no music was playing. Just the persistent tick of the tracking screen flashing the little green blimp the two were following. Tensions were high inside the vehicle. Alain dared not speak.

"What in the hell has he been doing? Who is this guy driving?"

"Well, at least we are finally on track to the seed Father Clementine planted into his mind. Do you think the friend is actually still living there?"

"How the hell should I know, Alain? It doesn't matter if the guy is there or not. We're setting him up to trap him and bring him to the Board of Directors."

"You know, we didn't actually set this trap up. We're just pieces in the plan."

"So, what's your point?"

"How do we know this is what we need to be doing?"

"Why would you of all people doubt the Board?"

"I'm not doubting the board. I just find it funny that they were able to get an operation into play so quickly."

"They probably already had it all laid out before we were even put on the assignment."

"Doesn't that bother you? That they are always so many steps ahead, it's almost as if they can read our thoughts."

"Not our thoughts, but our patterns. You know the math and science behind algorithms and how once the UN created the One Data Base there hasn't been much that can't be accurately predicted."

"Of course, I know the history. But recently, haven't you noticed there's been a drastic increase in the accuracy."

"Isn't that a good thing, Alain? Really, this is alarming coming from someone that is as loyal to the United Companies of America as you."

"My questions don't make me disloyal to the UCA," Alain snapped back.

"I didn't say that, Alain," Niki said measuring her tone and beginning to carefully choose which words to use next. "I think it's good the Board had this plan in place just in case we were unable to bring in Vladimir."

"Does that mean they think we're incompetent?"

"No. It just means that Vladimir Fortune is that damn good of an adversary. You know that better than anyone.

"As it stands, we don't truly know anything about the man named Vladimir Fortune. All we know is that he's a man the Board of Directors have been hunting for a long time."

"We know more than that, Alain."

"That's for us to know. The rest is our job."

"You really think there's a separation from the two?"

"As long as there is one in our mind and actions, yes."

"How naïve you are, Alain."

"You can call me naïve. We'll see who stands where when it is all said and done."

Niki felt the glare of Alain's gaze. She did not turn her head. Staring at the black pavement before her, Niki watched as the light reflectors blinked by in time with the little green blimp pinging Vladimir's signal.

◆

As Father Clementine continued to watch Vlad walk away, he continued his phone call.

"He is on his way," Father Clementine said into the phone never taking his eyes off of Vladimir. "Yes, the seed has been planted. Yes, the tracker is in place. Are you sure? No, I personally don't think they are the two that should handle this job. Of course, I would never disagree with the board. No. Well, you asked me what I think and that is what I am telling you. Take it for what it is worth. My allegiance to the Board of Directors is never in question. Do you understand me?"

There was a silence on the phone as the other person on the dial meditated on Father Clementine's words.

"Yes," the Father said. "I don't know what the plan is. Yes, I understand. Ok. I said I understand," Father Clementine said canceling the call with haste. The tingle of anger bubbled evenly as the lid of the Father's temper shook unstably, ready to pop.

Ishmael drove Vladimir to Marina Del Ray in the black Camry to the sounds of Manu Chao. Clandestino was the album of choice it seemed for this final voyage. Drifting lightly to the ticks and thumps drifting out of the speakers the two began to speak upon important things.

"So, what's the skinny?" Ishmael asked breaking the silence that had been floating comfortably.

"Excuse me?" Vlad asked genuinely confused.

"What's the story? I can tell by your aura that you're on the run."

"You can read auras?" Vlad asked beginning to feign sleep. He was beginning to think that linking up with this man Ishmael was a mistake.

"Yours ain't that difficult to read."

"How so?" Vlad asked taking the bait named intrigue.

"It's very obvious you're carrying around more than you can fill one life with. So that means you've had many lives."

"Ok."

"Am I correct?"

"Continue."

"I see. Thank you for the compliment."

"Who are you?"

"You know who I am. I am Ishmael."

"Ok then. Ishmael, how is it that you know of my past lives?"

"We all have past lives. That is the cycle of birth and death we are fortunate enough to endure. Saying that you have had your fill of lives, isn't much of a fortune telling. Most people on the street would agree if I said the same to them."

"Ok. So saying that is normal and we're just making conversation."

"You could say that. As I drive you to your destination. You could also say that, I owe you for doing me the favor and helping my wife and unborn child."

"You could say that. It'd be a bit unnecessary. Yet, I'd appreciate it. If that is the case, then how do you intend to deliver repayment for the favor I so graciously gifted to you."

"Look at you being all humble and shit."

"I have my moments."

"I'm sure you do. Repayment? Very simple really. All you have to do is listen to the guidance I am going to give to you, as I drive you to what I'm sure will be a key point in your already very long and confusing story."

Vladimir considered the driver Ishmael's offer, looking out the window as "La Primavera" played from the album 'Proxima Estacion: Esperanza' by Manu Chao. The sky was glittered with false illumination as lights stretched beyond what the eye could see. An imagination's worth of destruction packed into efficiency. Solving problems while giving birth to disasters. Life appeared pretty bleak. The Board of Directors ensured that the future seemed an almost definite end to humanity.

"I can agree to that," Vlad said boring himself with looking out the window. "Thank you."

Alain grew tired of staring at the blinking green blimp and took his eyes from the tracking device. Missing a right turn they should have taken, the two floated westward and away from Vladimir. Each was caught in the thought of their own hurt feelings. Niki couldn't allow herself to go beyond the frustration Alain aroused from within her. He always knew just how to get under her skin, Niki thought as she drove the Volkswagen farther away from where they were supposed to be.

"You know," Alain began, unable to endure the silence any longer. "There's a rest stop coming up. I need to use the toilet. Do you mind?"

"Are you serious, Alain? We're hunting an ex-convict just released from prison. We don't have time to take pit stops."

"It won't take us that far out of the way," Alain said glancing at the little green blinking blimp showing Vladimir's location. Realization pimp smacked Alain in the face taking his voice from his throat. They had gone off course. Now how was he to tell the already irritated beyond belief, Niki?

"Why'd you get so quiet?" she asked Alain.

Alain said nothing, staring into the tracking device as if it were a magic 8-ball. Contemplating nothing that came to mind, he suddenly started sweating inside of his white button up. The standard black suit and tie wasn't helping one bit either.

"Alain, what's wrong?"

Left with no choice, Alain had to spill the beans. "We missed our mark?"

"What do you mean we missed our mark?" Niki asked nostrils flaring.

"I mean, we missed a turn and now we're about 20 minutes outside the radius."

"20 minutes," Niki said smashing the breaks bringing the car to a halt. "Are you fucking kidding me, Alain?! How the hell did you let this happen?"

"I guess I missed it somehow, I'm not sure," Alain could feel his heart shrinking as his stomach filled with intestine eating butterflies.

"You're not sure?!" Niki asked him. "You're not sure?" she repeated the question disappearing from her tone.

A great weight began to flood into the car, increasing the pressure upon Alain. At that moment a giant thunderclap erupted from the sky. After a few startled moments later, rain began to cascade down. A few cars swerved around the halted Volkswagen switching lanes unable to handle the torrential down pour. Niki's anger seethed as she took her foot from the brake and accelerated the car forward on the highway, 40 miles from the nearest exit.

◆ ◆ ◆

All the way on the other side of the country. In Company 50, what used to be called New York, the Board of Directors sat huddled around a large table. Sitting high atop the 200th floor of the tallest tower in the UC of A, the board of 12 talked over one another and were engaged in their daily pursuit of pretending to do business. Commander Bryant sat at the head of the large table eyeing each of the 11 board members that made up the other 49% of decisions made for the future of the Company Security Division. Commander Bryant held the majority 51% of decision-making power for the CSD.

Watching the ducks' squabble in a row grew tiresome for the seasoned commander. He rose from his chair and walked out of the room, unnoticed. Trekking down the long hallway leading to the central elevators, Commander Bryant swam through his memory log of the past three days. There wasn't much that he hadn't already searched through. He didn't even know what he was looking for really. Swimming through the memory log was an old habit he had developed from his father, the Great Admiral Granite.

"Always look through your memory log," Commander Bryant's father had told him the first time when he was seven. The two were hiking, beyond the rim, and there was zero room for error there. Non-authorized personnel were not allowed to wander beyond the rim. Admiral Granite was fully aware of this rule as he himself was the one that set it. The Admiral, however, was also the individual in charge to say whom was or was not authorized to transverse the forbidden land. This was of course for the protection of the citizens. From the Beast.

No one really knew what the beast were. The few fortunate souls able to make it back from beyond the rim spoke of four legged creatures reminiscent of the wolf species that went extinct ten years ago. No one knew either why the beast stayed beyond the rim. Never venturing past the border line that is the forest, the beast stalked the perimeter ready to pounce upon whomever stepped foot beyond the rim.

"Why do we have to always look through our memory log, father?" the seven-year-old Bryant asked his father, the newly appointed Great Admiral of the CSD. The forest was coming to an end and the expanse of land that used to be known as Mexico stretched as desert before the father and son.

Admiral Granite stopped his son from walking and turned toward him. There was no easy way to say this.

"Son, you have to always look through your memory log, because The Tribunal erases what you remember."

"I don't understand, father. I thought The Tribunal protected us."

"They do not. It is of the utmost importance that you understand this."

"Father, I'm confused. Don't you work for the Tribunal?"

"I work for the Company Security Division. There is a very distinct difference that you will soon come to understand when you go to the Academy."

The very thought of departing the only reality the seven-year-old Bryant had ever known, was not something that catered well to the imagination of the Admiral's son. Sensing the fear building in his seed, Great Admiral Granite put his hand on Bryant's right shoulder and squeezed.

As he reached the elevator to the main lobby, Commander Bryant could swear he felt that squeeze. Well that's something I won't be sharing with anyone, he thought to himself as the elevators opened and welcomed an empty lift. The hyper transport shot Commander Bryant's stomach into his throat and his lungs ceased to work. Just as his eyes began to bulge from their sockets a soft ding chimed overhead and the elevator doors opened on the lobby floor. 200 floors were just too many, Commander Bryant thought stepping out with wobbly legs onto the lobby.

The lunch traffic had started and CSD workers everywhere were busying themselves in lonely clumps of 3s and 4s mostly, with an occasional group of one, deciding what to eat for the allotted hour. Commander Bryant dodged the mass of people darting back and forth and exited the CSD headquarters located in Company 50, previously known as New York.

The air quality was marked as below 30% which meant oxygen tanks, for those that could afford them, weren't necessary. Nevertheless, Commander Bryant strapped on his O2 mask and breathed in the artificial air. As his father, Admiral Granite, had taught him. He never trusted the air of any of the Company's.

Clean air was a commodity the UCA had never known.

As he walked down the street it began to rain. A sizzle could be heard as Commander Bryant's skin began to tinge from the acid drizzling down from the scorched sky. Company 50 had by far the worst atmosphere in America. Tapping the implant tucked away into the corner under his ear, Commander Bryant activated his rain coat. A layer of latex skin suddenly coated his entire body. Glancing at his watch he decided it best to hop in a taxi. It didn't take much to hail one.

"Where to, Commander?" Commander Bryant appreciated the subtle privileges of rank in a country owned by companies. Following the 3rd revolt, the country became a military state and Commander Bryant and his father shot to heroic status overnight.

"You can take me to the Civic Center," Commander Bryant finally answered the cab driver.

"You got it, sir."

As the taxi careened down the highway, Commander Bryant returned to that first trip beyond the rim with his father Great Admiral Granite.

The two were on a father son adventure. They had been playing the game since Commander Bryant was able to walk. Their father son adventures were what solidified Commander Bryant's mind that he was going to follow in the footsteps of his highly decorated dad.

The implant tucked in the corner of his ear began to vibrate. Touching his finger on the tingling implant, Commander Bryant activated his receiver. After the soft beep sounded confirming connection, a voice came forth.

"Incoming transmission from the CSD."

"Accept," Commander Bryant said leaning his head toward the side window and looking up at the scorched sky. The light from the sun could be seen through the dome of pollution engulfing the sky. The taxi bouncing along the road swaying him to and fro' calmed Commander Bryant in anticipation of whatever the hell was to come on the call.

"This is Corporal Boon."

"Good afternoon, Corporal. How can I be of assistance?"

"I just wanted to inform you that, Vladimir Fortune was released from ROX prison earlier today."

"Yes, I received the briefing this morning. He should be en route to HQ for his full memory sweep."

"Vladimir Fortune has escaped his handlers, sir."

The calm serenity that had been tempting to take over Commander Bryant sharply snatched itself away, leaving behind seething anger.

"Please repeat, Corporal."

"As of 43 minutes ago, Vladimir Fortune has gone missing."

"Who are his handlers?"

A slight hesitation from the Corporal was all it took for Commander Bryant to know exactly who was responsible.

"Niki Brown and her husband Alain Machado," Corporal Boon answered.

Commander Bryant scrunched up his face in irritation and clenched his teeth tightly together.

"I thought I advised, quite adamantly, that the two of them were to be suspended from any field operations for the duration of their individual pending investigations."

"You did, sir. And the board truly did take your concerns into consideration. However, it was decided that given the close relations between agent Niki Brown and Vladimir Fortune it would be beneficial for her to coerce the mark into the green zone."

"That's the dumbest assessment you could've possibly made. Are you kidding me?" Commander Bryant asked dumbfounded.

"Yes, sir. In retrospect the board regrets not following your recommendation."

"I bet it does," Commander Bryant said hanging up the call on Corporal Boon. Fucking imbeciles, he thought to himself as the taxi headed toward the Civic Center. Once there he hopped from the taxi tossing a solid tip behind him. The Civic Center's bronze towers grasped beyond infinity it would seem. The three tall buildings that made up the CSD were filled 100 floors deep with thousands of workers.

Commander Bryant was in charge of all of them.

"Evening, Commander," the guard at the front desk said as he walked into the building lobby. Trading one lobby for another, he thought as he looked at the guard.

"Evening, sir," Commander Bryant responded. "How are things today?"

"So-so. The members of the Tribunal left about 30 minutes ago. I wasn't expecting anyone to be coming in today. Is everything alright, sir?"

Always the nosy body Commander Bryant smiled to himself at the guard's curiosity. "There's not much going on really. Just a lot of paper work that needs to be done."

"Don't you have people to do that for you?"

"Of course. That doesn't mean I can't do work to. It needs to get done and honestly, I can do it quicker 'cause I know more about what's going on. I make the things that are classified, classified."

"Damn, that makes sense. Well, that's good you have the mindset to roll up your sleeves and do it. I'm definitely sure you don't have to."

"If I want thoroughness I do. And occasionally I happen upon some very superb work from some intern that's grinding away and churning out gold."

"What do you do with them?"

"Promote them and change their entire meaning of existence. I also find a lot of people fucking up.

"And what do you do with those people?"

"Fire them," Commander Bryant said scanning his key card and walking through the electronic barriers preventing non-card members from entering.

"And that's why you're here going into work."

"Exactly," Commander Bryant said with a wave of two fingers. There wasn't much left for him to say. Off he went towards the elevators and before he knew it, he was on the 300th floor overlooking Company 50. A sad sight laid itself before the son of Admiral Granite. The scorched sky above painted a portrait of hopelessness that almost stole the heart of Commander Bryant. A century worth of war had left a significant number of slaves to injustice nourished by the Tribunal. Just as his father had taught him, Commander Bryant quickly changed the flow of his thoughts and made a mental record to erase his sightseeing pause from his memory when he got home.

"There hasn't been a whole lot that's been done right!" Commander Bryant hollered into the phone. "As far as I'm concerned, each of you is responsible for letting a terrorist run free. There isn't a single thing your incompetent board can do now to assist the CSD. Understand me, ladies and gentlemen. I am taking control of this operation and from now until the day I say so, control is in the hands of myself. Do you understand?"

As expected, the room of holograms representing the board members all nodded in consent.

"Very well then. Now, what was his last known sighting?"

It took a few seconds for Niki Brown to chime in.

"The last point of contact with Vladimir Fortune was near the Bus Station on Belmont, just beyond the Orange Bridge."

"I think it's safe to assume he's crossed over the Orange Bridge. So that means he's made his way into the 'Ghetto.'"

"Why would anyone in their right minds voluntarily go into the 'ghetto?'?" Sherrie the newest of the board members asked. She quickly realized her slip, a moment too late for the taste of Commander Bryant, who snatched her tongue with lightening ferocity.

Holding the warm organ in his hands, Commander Bryant took a bite from it, and continued on.

"The Ghetto is the best place to hide. As long as you ask permission from the Elders. He who enters without permission, seeks a swift death savagely laid out with great indifference. It'll take him a day to get that permission."

Commander Bryant glanced at his Hamilton wrist watch.

"That gives us 12 hours to activate every asset we have in the Ghetto and see about putting Vladimir Fortune down once and for all."

Scanning the room for weakness, Commander Bryant found much. Tossing aside the observation, all urgency began to tackle the task at hand. The hunt was on. This is what I do best Commander Bryant thought to himself as he closed his eyes and daydreamed on the chase.

The moving image of his wife flashed by gently raising his life. At that moment, Commander Bryant's wife was in Company 1 arguing policy to a congress that would never listen to her. Company 1 used to be called Washington DC, and frankly not much has changed.

"Gentlemen," Commander Bryant's wife Justine shouted out to the assembly barking incoherently before her. "It would seem that we have come to an impasse. At this juncture I would like to call for a halt to these, deliberations, and reconvene at a later date when the gentlemen present aren't as…flustered by the presence of a woman."

Justine's statement did very little to soothe the hurt egos of the assembly made up of 14 men over the age of 200. Pockets of chatter broke out causing the highest council in the United Companies of America to fill with the sound of chicken's squawking. Justine stood before the council unswaying in her poise. Silence and stubbornness alone quieted the room.

"Thank you for your attention, kind sirs," Justine said after allowing the snatch of stillness to waft into each one of the assemblymen's hearts. None dared utter a sound. The power Justine welded wasn't something she used often. Just enough so as to remind people what she is.

"My species," Justine continued elevating her voice to oratory perfection. "The Tungalao, as humans have deemed to classify us. We have been cast out of our homes and made to follow your laws since the discovery of our sanctuary."

"You mean the discovery of your hideout," barked one of the men representing Company 14 home of the windy city.

"It was our sanctuary. As you know, we had fled the revolutions that took place before humans walked the planet and had no intention of ever returning to the surface."

"You all were plotting to take back the land you all claim to used to be yours millions of years ago. The very notion of which is laughable, and amazingly kind of the Tribunal to entertain all this time. Bottom line, you all have been treated as first class guests and now you're sitting here asking for the right to participate in our election process. To hold a seat at the Tribunal. To have the opportunity to even be president. The arrogance of such a request baffles us all. I am the only one brave enough to say it to your face, however."

Justine calmly listened to the squabbling of the representative from Company 14. There wasn't much to expect from Company 14. Historically corrupt and home to notoriety, Justine had no intentions of putting up a fight to try and convince any of these men to understand the plight of her species. She didn't need them to understand. She needed them to sign over voting rights to the Tungalao, as they like to call us, Justine thought.

"I believe we have heard enough for today," the speaker finally rose and spoke, silencing the entire audience. "We will honor the councilwoman's request and halt discussion for today. Meeting is adjourned ladies and gentlemen.

"Thank you very much, sir," Justine said over the loud calmer of everyone leaving. Her bow of respect for the Tribunal went unnoticed to all in the room. Watching the preceding's through video feed, the President saw Justine's bow, and it intrigued him deeply.

◆ ◆ ◆

Just as Justine's meeting was ending and her husband Commander Bryant was being informed of Vladimir Fortunes unknown whereabouts, Vlad arrived at the Marine to see his friend Quincy. Ishmael gave some parting words of advice and drove off back to his very pregnant wife. The marine was gorgeous.

Boats lined as far as the eye could see. The sun was just cracking over the horizon, sending its orange hue throughout the sky. As Vlad had expected, how or why he did not know, Quincy was easily found. Almost in the exact same spot they had parted ways 12 years prior. Vlad's friend Quincy was smoking from a wooden pipe laying on his back staring up at the sky in the back of his boat.

"Yo," Vlad said as way of greeting.

Quincy didn't budge. Just went on smoking the oak wood pipe. Vlad remembered when he got the pipe. It was a divorce gift from Quincy's second wife. That was more than 12 years ago, Vlad thought as he watched Quincy either sleep or ignore him.

"Yo," Vlad finally called again. "Get up, fool," he said finally hopping onto the boat and kicking Quincy in the leg. Quincy startled and opened his eyes. Unsurprised as always, Quincy smiled when his vision made out his friend Vladimir staring down at him.

After embracing and passing the pipe back and forth a few times, Quincy invited Vlad into his living quarters. The gentle sway of the boat rocking eased the tension Vlad had been carrying. As he plopped down onto the sofa to the left of the opening, Quincy handed him a beer.

"Thanks," Vlad said pulling the ring atop the can opening the beer. The satisfying fizz sounded and Quincy's own beer followed suit, echoing.

"So, when'd you get out?" Quincy asked.

"Yesterday, I guess. Or the day before that."

"A lot has happened since then, I see," Quincy said falling down beside Vlad on the coach and taking sips of beer.

"Yea, you could say that?"

"Know why they let you out?"

"Yep, sure do. 'Cause, from what everyone seems to think, including me; I may be immortal."

"Well, you're not really immortal. There just doesn't seem to be a broken narrative in your memories of past lives. You do die. What happens to you, according to what belief you look at, isn't all that unusual. Reincarnation is a perspective that's been around for hundreds of thousands of years. Most people just don't remember their previous lives."

"Well, whatever that is. That's why they want to put me in a facility."

"To dissect and study you."

"Yea, like I'm some kind of alien."

"Have you ever considered that you just might be? "Quincy said pushing play on the game controller he had grabbed off the treasure chest sitting in front of us. 'Hotel California' by the Eagles began to play through the speakers he had tucked away somewhere in the small quarters that was his boat, called the 'Little Getta.'

◆

In a flash, our dear hero was stuck in a loop of forgotten memory. Over and over again, Vladimir tumbled deeper into his psyche. There was no way to get out, so committing to the dive was the only thing left for him to do. With a splash that sent ripples of recollections into motion all grew from the one stream of the fall.

Swimming his way to the surface of the giant body of water, Vladimir found himself in, once at the top he saw that he was in the middle of the ocean. There was no land in sight as the waves vigorously bobbed him from side to side up and down and all around. Salt water hit his lips and poured into his mouth. Vladimir couldn't stop swallowing sea water and became afraid he was going to drown. He didn't even know how he had ended up there.

Quincy slapped his friend in the shoulder pulling him out of the ocean in his mind Vladimir had found himself having fallen into.

"Thanks," he said to Quincy taking a swig of beer.

"Did I ever tell you about my great uncle, Clarence?" Quincy asked

"I don't think so."

"He lived during the country when it was going through segregation, before the Companies."

"That was a very long time ago."

"Yes, it was. I never met the man obviously, but I was told lots of stories about him and other relatives."

"That's crazy your family kept records like that."

"Yea, you're right it is."

Just then, Vlad coughed violently until blood projectile vomited from his mouth onto the wooden floor of his friend Quincy's boat. The nano-bytes that he knew nothing about had succeed in fatally wounding him. The pain made Vladimir collapse from the sofa and his muscles uncontrollably convulsed away. Quincy watched as his friend Vladimir Fortune died horribly.

It didn't take very long for the CSD to show up. Commander Bryant was surgically precise and located Vlad from satellite imaging in a matter of moments after receiving the call from Corporal Boon that he had escaped custody. They bagged up and transported his body before Quincy even realized what was happening. Efficiency to its highest degree. As night fell the boat seemed empty to Quincy. He laid on his back staring at the stars, smoking the oak wood pipe, wondering what life his friend Vladimir was on his way to being born into.

The entity that use to be Vladimir knew that was not the way the rebirth process worked. The darkness and then relief were the first things it felt as the life force of Vladimir Fortune ceased to be. How it had missed the feeling of freedom. Real freedom could never be felt while trapped in the human form. No, only when rejoining the universe could all-encompassing freedom be had. Yet, it had to admit as it floated along unable to control, not thinking or doing; being human was beyond great and always the opportunity the universe seeks.

There were no judgments nor reading off of all the good and bad things done in the previous life lived. There wasn't even memory. It was something beyond nothing that encapsulates everything. No being or existing, just …..

Then came the plunge back into life. It was like being snatched out of a line for no reason and tossed into a dryer at the laundry mat. 'Round and 'round it went until singular awareness emerged. To the surprise of the entity, a plethora of memory shot into whatever it was in the process of becoming. Apparently, there were still more lives left to live.

The pool of discomfort was similar to that old feeling not felt for over a lifetime. Going from nothing to something and forming into a human being is almost as painful as dying for the 20th time, Vladimir Fortune thought. As the child bursts from his 21st mother's womb, he looks around the room, shuttered at the thought of how long it would take before it could even talk. Looking into the eyes of the doctor as she handed the newborn to its mother, the entity that once was Vlad knew more than the PhD would ever gain. But for right now, it was just a baby.

"Congratulations," the doctor said to the mother that had just given birth. You have a beautiful baby girl.

I'm a baby girl, the entity that once was and never will be again, Vladimir, thought as she was bundled up in a soft pink blanket and handed over to her mother. The heart she had been listening to for 9 months beat out a luba-dub-dub of familiarity. The baby girl that was just born calmed quickly and settled comfortably between her mother's bosom.

Mother and daughter both dozed off from exhaustion. Time, space, and dimension had shift and once again the entity that used to be

Vladimir Fortune, began a brand-new life in a brand-new realm for the 21st time.

Flying back to the time and place where Vladimir's body is getting cold in a morgue. Commander Bryant is seen standing over the autopsy table. Observing the doctor's accurate procedure, he was seething in anger.

"How are we ever going to find him again?" Commander Bryant asked to the cold room, startling the doctor. The two stood frozen as the echo of the Commander's voice reverberated through its course toward silence. "Sorry about that. I didn't mean to scare you."

"That's alright," the doctor said putting down his scalpel then removing his mask and gloves. Commander Bryant glanced at the blade.

"Is that blade encrusted with diamonds?"

"It is made out of a diamond," the doctor said throwing the gloves and mask in the biohazardous waste basin. "I brought it back from, China. Let me show you what I was able to find," the doctor said motioning for Commander Bryant to come toward the eyes.

"How'd you get out of the United Companies?"

"I'm a very good surgeon," the doctor said opening the body of Vladimir Fortune's eye lids.

Resigned to let that comment from the surgeon performing the autopsy flutter away, Commander Bryant gave his attention to the doctor. "What do you got for me?" he asked.

"Ever since you brought this case of, the entity that can remember past lives, to me I have been hard at work developing a way to track those past lives as best as we can."

"We've already determined that there is no scientific way to trace any of those lives back," Commander Bryant responded beginning to become irritated for having his time wasted.

The doctor continued talking uninterrupted and without halting from the procedure he was showing Commander Bryant. Grabbing ahold of the diamond scalpel he had sat down a few moments ago, along with a new set of gloves and mask. The doctor began to slice along the body of Vladimir Fortune's eyelids. Removing them from the body, it stared up at the sky with dead eyes.

"I've been developing a theory for a while that I believe could help you get a step closer in your search and understanding of this phenomenal entity the Tribunal has taken such a passionate interest in."

"I'm all ears, of course," Commander Bryant said forced through desperation to listen to every crack pot idea that came his way.

"Well, you see it's very simple. We each have an implant located in our brains just behind our eyes. This works for so many things in our society today. You in essence can't even survive, at least in our country, without the implant."

"Doctor, you're telling me things I already know," Commander Bryant said glancing at his Hamilton wrist watch.

"Of course, how silly of me. As you know very well, I'm sure, one of the main functions of the implant is to store memory. It's designed to store a lifetime's worth and depending upon the individual, what's stored in the implant could be worth millions or billions even."

"Yes, you're very right about that. But there are incredibly strict laws against tampering with unauthorized implants and all are wiped clean upon death."

"For those bodies we are able to get access to. The Company Security Division does a stand-up job of getting ahold of most bodies. But you know as well as I, Commander Bryant, that demand for implants is high in the black market."

"So, what are you getting at?" Commander Bryant said with a tone of losing patience.

"I've developed, maybe, a way to play back the lives the entity remembers when it existed within this body."

"How do we know it even thought about its past lives?"

"Because we know it can remember them," the doctor said removing the body of Vladimir fortune's implant from the blood hole of a mess he had been working on while talking to Commander Bryant. I don't think it has much of a choice but to remember these lives."

"There isn't a machine that can play lives to be watched like a movie, doctor. I'm not sure the technology exists to be perfectly honest."

"You're right, it doesn't. So far, the only way available to view recorded data is through code and then translation of that into words or visuals or both. But I've invented a way to watch on a screen the memories of the implant."

"Why haven't you shared this with anyone yet? You could be very rich."

"It's still in the prototype phase. I'm only able to sustain enough power to run the program for 2 minutes and I haven't been able to access the main index of the memories."

"So there just coming randomly and you aren't able to control any kind of access?"

"Correct. We can watch them; we just don't know what the hell we're watching."

"And for the entity, that could be a Pandora's Box of memories over a dozen or more lifetimes."

"We don't know how many lives the entity has lived through?"

"We don't know very much about the entity at all, to be honest. What we do know is from observations collected while it was living life as Vladimir Fortune. It's popped up in a few random places throughout history and time, but it's more than likely the concept. There were others that were able to remember past lives as well just like the one we've been chasing."

"You really believe there are others?"

"I believe anything until its proven false to me," Commander Bryant said. "Show me this machine you've invented."

"With pleasure, Commander. Right this way."

It took the doctor about 20 minutes to get cleaned up and another 30 to drive to the warehouse where he kept his laboratory. Commander

Bryant nodded his head in approval at the tenacity of this doctor he was becoming more and more fascinated to know.

After watching the demonstration, Commander Bryant was sold. His mind began to race.

"Do you have the entity's implant?" the Commander asked once he was able to gain control of his streaming thoughts.

The doctor pulled from his green scrubs pocket a small plastic evidence bag containing Vladimir Fortune's implant. They both smiled in anticipation as the machine was set up.

"Ok, let's see what comes out first," the doctor said pressing play as they both looked up at the screen.

The first image was that of a small girl tucked into bed. She had her nighty-time clothes on and seemed to be sleeping that peaceful sleep we wish for all children to keep. The image passed a mirror and we see a younger version of Vladimir Fortune.

"Vlad," a voice calls from the bed. The images on the screen the doctor and Commander Bryant are watching shift from the mirror and return to the bed. The little girl is seen now awake and sitting upright.

"What are you doing awake?" the young voice of Vladimir Fortune is heard for the first time. The screen moves over to the bed and sits down on it.

"I heard you come in," the little girl responds moving over and making room for Vladimir to sit on the bed next to her. A hand appears we are to assume is Vladimir's in this memory data from the implant the doctor extracted earlier.

"Is everything ok?" the voice of young Vladimir asked the little girl.

"I had a bad dream," she responded rubbing her sleepy eyes and looking cuter than a button. Even though buttons aren't really that cute, Commander Bryant thought to himself as he watched the scene of Vladimir's memory unfold.

The young Vladimir got into bed with the little girl and the two drifted off to sleep. Questions swam through Commander Bryant's brain. Very little was known of Vladimir Fortune's background. He could not recall if she was a daughter or a younger sister. Who was this little girl?

After some time passed, the doctor and Commander Bryant watched the young Vladimir Fortune snake his arm from under the little girl he helped go back to sleep. He tiptoed out of the room and then the screen went white.

"What happened?!" Commander Bryant barked out louder than he had intended. "I'm sorry," he quickly said catching himself.

"That's quite alright," the doctor replied messing around with the machine. "As I told you earlier, we only have enough power to run a memory back 2 minutes at a time."

"And we can't return to that frame?"

"As of now, no. I have been unable to figure out how to access the mainframe of the implant."

"No table of contents."

"Precisely."

"How long does it take to upload another memory?"

"I'm almost done loading another one now. Shall I start the playback?"

"Yes," Commander Bryant replied intently focusing on the large screen before him. "How do we know if what we're watching is a memory of this life or one of the entity's previous ones?"

"We don't," the doctor replied shaking his head in frustration. "This is one of the incredibly many questions I have been unable to find the answers to."

"Well, now you have my assistance. I have the access to get you whatever you need to make this machine of yours 100%"

"You're not understanding," the doctor said pushing play on the playback. "The technology doesn't exist to accomplish what we must."

"Then I guess you're going to have to invent it, doctor," Commander Bryant said leaning back in the chair he sat in and watched the screen as the next memory began.

The way dreams often do, starting in the midst of action, the playback of the entity that was Vladimir Fortune's memory started in a classroom. A male teacher was droning on about something. It took a moment for the scene before them to be understood by the Commander and doctor.

"And who among you can tell us why it is that Melville writes so obsessively of the whaling experience?" the teacher asked in a shrill pitched voice.

The eyes through which the doctor and Commander Bryant are observing the scene before them dart around the room. No hands of any student are seen raised.

"Come on ladies and gentlemen. It was in your text you were supposed to have read last night."

"That doesn't mean we know what you're talking about, coach," came a voice from the corner. The classroom of teenagers erupted in laughter.

"Mr. Sanders, would you mind refraining from ejaculating comments off the field?" the teacher asked in a robust and load voice that echoed around the classroom. Her use of the word ejaculate, however, caused an even larger uproar of laughter to bellow from the student's throats.

"Yes, Ms. Pepper," the teacher called on the girl in the third row near the left, which was near the window. Her long arm stretched high toward the florescent lights skating the ceiling. The camera image swayed quickly to the right to zero in on the voice speaking. A red headed woman with freckles and pink skin took up the screen before the doctor and Commander. She wasn't beautiful, this teenage student. But she did command the classroom just as she pulled the gaze of the two men watching Vladimir fortune's memory.

The implant technology was something that had come about one hundred years prior to Vladimir Fortune's death. It was a pretty natural progression after Steve Jobs introduced the concept of a smart phone that attached itself onto the ever-self-centered aspect of human nature that could possibly be imagined. At no fault his own. When the implants were introduced in 2039, it was no stretch that the masses of humanity in a time period of 15 years all signed up for the procedure. A simple 20-minute surgery was all it took and in the blink of an eye every citizen legally and illegally in the entire United Companies of America, was connected to the mainframe from birth. Only an implant grants entry into the UCA.

Commander Bryant zeroed in on the screen. Ms. Pepper extrapolated her answer as a teacher's pet does best.

"Melville's intent was to share the enlightenment he obtained through whaling. By putting so much detail in he is able to provide the reader with everything needed to fully grasp the story being laid out as authentically as a whaler would."

The 'end of class' bell sounded and the words of the teenage student floated away in the commotion of kids gathering their things and hastening their way out of the classroom. The screen's image showing the memories of Vladimir Fortune as he saw them happen through his eyes stayed on Ms. Pepper as she slowly gathered her books into her bag. Sadness glowed forth from her as Vladimir's gaze did not divert. As tears gathered and began to fall from her eye lids, the screen went blank and the two minutes of playback elapsed.

# Chapter Three:
## Thought Therapy

Commander Bryant sat watching playback after playback. It consumed him for the next 20 years. There was a lifetimes worth of memories in Vladimir Fortune's implant and each of those memories were windows into other lifetimes.

The doctor improved the machine as each year passed and the two formed a bond built upon the Entity's past. Bouncing through multitudes of dimensions and realms upon realms, time itself seemed to be the only constant marching through the stories Commander Bryant watched.

And then he came upon Vladimir's sessions with me, his thought therapist.

◆ ◆ ◆

# A BRIEF HISTORY OF THOUGHT THERAPY

Amid the turmoil of the first collapse, the search for authenticity was rampant. Authenticity of self, authenticity of society, and authenticity of thoughts words and deeds. It was the thoughts that became of primary importance after the introduction of the implant into the free market. Once government approval was obtained, it didn't take long for an entire generation of parents to inject their newborns with the device. A smart phone in head, that does so much more, is how they advertised it. How such a thing sounded desirable I will never understand.

Approaching a breaking point in the first versions, a pending lawsuit brought forth the discovery of the importance thoughts played on the implants. Latching onto any negativity, the implants intensified the imaginations of the subject and often, depending upon then nature of the thoughts, drove them insane. As the cases of insanity rose it became apparent to the Tribunal that something needed to be done to restore peace of mind to the populace.

After consulting with top psychologists and psychiatrists, a new method of treatment was created specifically for individuals with implants. This is where thought therapy comes in.

In the beginning, access to the mind was obtained through technological means. These methods branched out into infinite spider webs of innovation, helping society cope with the freedoms that had been taken from them. It didn't take long for machines to become addicting, and product makers ceased to care about the mental health benefits, they went with what produced maximum profit. As of all things in a capitalistic society, thought therapy sought through technology became another pharmaceutical creating more harm than good.

Alongside the advancements in technology, there was a smaller field of study that was doing just as much, if not more, remarkable work simultaneously. This was the field of telepathic thought therapy.

The first known records of telepathic thought therapy date back to ancient Egypt. There were scatters of light-evidence throughout the next few millennia. However, nothing conclusive could ever be proven that telepathic thought therapy had been a viable form of medicine, before its introduction as a practice by Dr. John Whittle.

Dr. John Whittle had spent a large portion of his life in self-imposed exile on a non-extradition island somewhere near the south China Seas. It was during this hiatus that he developed the practice of thought therapy. It is unclear how Dr. Whittle came to possess the ability and wisdom to harness thought therapy into a scientific study.

When he returned to civilization, Dr. Whittle began transmitting his teachings immediately. It didn't take long for the pharmaceutical companies to interject their traps and before long Thought Therapy was primarily administered through mechanic and chemical means. Thought Therapy fell far from the grace to which Dr. Whittle brought via the evolution of psychology. Once government controlled and regulated, Thought Therapy lost its essence and became another device of surveillance and control in the UCA.

◆ ◆ ◆

When Commander Bryant stepped into my office, I would later learn he had been engrossed in the playback memories of Vladimir Fortune, and his many lives, for 7 ½ years. He looked old, haggard and tired. Not having much experience with Military personnel, I had no reason to think anything of his appearance when we met.

"Dr. Leon Cane?" Commander Bryant inquired as we shook hands.

"Yes," I replied, squeezing his hand and looking into his eyes.

"I was wondering if you could help me with something." Commander Bryant said providing a professional glimpse at his badge and getting right down to business.

"Yes, of course," I said, motioning for him and his deputy that stood at attention behind him to enter the office. "Please, sit down. So, how can I help you, Commander?"

"Well, you could start by talking about a client of yours, Vladimir Fortune."

"I was informed to believe that Vladimir Fortune unfortunately met his demise some years ago," I remember saying, wishing I had poured glasses of water when the Commander and deputy had entered my work place. Caught off guard as I was, there wasn't much reason to lie. I answered forthcoming.

"Yes, Vladimir Fortune is dead. However, there is a matter of great importance concerning his past that I believe you can help the United Companies with."

"I see. This is for the companies?" I asked with a skeptical smile.

"Yes, it is Dr. Cane," Commander Bryant said to me. His tone turned my veins to ice.

"How exactly can I help you?" I asked shaking the frost from my lungs.

"I need you to tell me all that you know about Vladimir Fortune. Everything that he spoke of from the moment you met him, until the very last session you had before hearing about your patient's untimely death."

"You know I can't do that, Commander. The confidentiality laws are very clear when it comes to this."

"Dr. Cane, this is for national security. I believe you know the severity of the crimes committed by Vladimir Fortune."

"Regardless, he is dead. Therefore, any investigation is just to appease your sad ego that seems to have gotten the better of you. As a therapist, Commander, I would recommend you seek therapy."

"I'll take you up on that, Doctor. But first, I will need your help. It is for national security and not to appease my ego, I assure you. Now, if you will, doctor; I'd appreciate it if you started from the beginning and tell me everything you recall from your encounters with Vladimir Fortune. Do you think you can do that, Dr. Leon Cane?"

Left with no options but to comply, I nodded my head with as much dignity as I could muster and tapped the implant behind my ear to access the files being sought.

◆

"Vladimir Fortune first stepped into my office three years before he was put in prison. He got my number from a patron that frequented the same bar as he did. I guess the two got to talking about racing thoughts and wanting to control their minds. The patron that recommended me to Vlad has since went on to seek alternative help. I assume she's doing well. Vladimir came to the office in the morning and made an appointment in person, so I squeezed him in for that same evening. What he unloaded onto me was more than I could ever have imagined. I was sure he was absolutely crazy the first twenty minutes of our session. But then as he continued, I couldn't help but believe that he truly was remembering his past lives, and it was driving him crazy."

"Do you have any audio recordings of your sessions?" Commander Bryant asked me.

"Yes, of course. I recorded every session," I said rising from where I sat. I pulled out a box from the closest, tucked away behind the open door. I always keep the doors open in thought therapy sessions.

"What's this?" Commander Bryant asked beginning to rummage through the box I tossed on top of the desk.

"These are all the tapes from every session I have ever had with Vladimir."

"Why did you already have them sorted out of the rest?"

"Commander Bryant, you're here because whatever Vladimir Fortune was still exists now. And it scares the hell out of you."

"That's true."

"You should listen to the tapes, I'll set up the playback for you. Would you like a drink? You look like you could use one."

Commander Bryant stared at me, unblinking. The poor man had fallen into the maze of seeking out Vladimir Fortune's past lives.

**TAPE #1**

"Testing, testing, one-two. Testing one-two. This is Dr. Leon Cane speaking. Would you please state your name for the record?"

"Vladimir Fortune."

"Thank you very much Vladimir. You entered into these offices of your own accord. Is that correct?"

"Yes, that's correct."

"Very good, very good. Now, what can I do for you today, Vladimir?"

"I'm not very sure if you can help me actually."

"Well, let's just see if we can help in some way. What primarily has brought you into my office?"

"My thoughts are made up of memories that span over a dozen past lives. I can remember every single one of my past lives."

"I'm not sure that I follow you?"

"Do you believe that life is eternal?"

"Yes, I guess I could say that I do."

"Well, as we all live out our lives and are reborn into others, we sporadically have glimpses of feeling, echoes of semblance. These remind us often of far reaching things, worlds we haven't the full courage to admit exist in our minds."

"Deja vu?"

"In a way, yes. However, I can remember vividly my past lives the way most people remember their experiences in grade school."

"I'm not sure I can believe that to be true."

"Some days, I'm not entirely sure it to be true either. That's why I'm here, you see. I've been bouncing from life to life for too long now.

The narrative hasn't run out but my spirit can't quite seem to take it. And this world, this life now, it's a bit worse off than all the other 18 lives I've walked the entirety of."

"What do you mean?"

"It's hard to pinpoint it. There's just a sense of resignation that I've only felt in this life. All my other lives, in the different realms and worlds and dimensions, contained a glimmer of hope somewhere. This world though, from the moment I was born into it I knew. It's a plastic world where the fabrications became currency for the soul."

Silence can be heard stretching its gait from the recording being played.

"Why don't we start from the beginning," Dr. Leon Cane can be heard saying. "When did you first come to recognize you could remember your past lives?"

"The farthest back I can remember is 18 lives, I think. A lot of what I'm going on is assumption derived through feeling."

"Naturally."

"I'm pretty certain I've had many lives before that point. Just for some reason it's primarily there that I can remember from. That first life that I could remember past lives is like the beginning of existence for my narrative."

"What makes you sure you had lives before that one?"

"Symptom of my own personal religious beliefs."

"And those are?"

"I'm a Buddhist."

"Were you a Buddhist in all of your lives?"

"I wasn't born into Buddhist families, if that's what you mean. But I did have a family that was Buddhist."

"In one of your lives you were born into a Buddhist family?"

"Right. It helped me get a better understanding of what was going on with me. In terms of bouncing from life to life remembering everything."

"Ok, so. You'll understand if I have a lot of questions for you."

"Yes," the voice of young Vladimir Fortune said. Silence once again popped its presence into the recording as Commander Bryant and the (Deputy) standing at attention behind him sat and listened captivated by the thought therapy sessions Dr. Cane was allowing them to hear.

"Ok, first of all," Dr. Cane abruptly started up again. "I take this as you believe that this is happening and therefore it is very real to you. However, I cannot fully cosign onto the fact that you have even had past lives, nor that you can remember them."

"That's fair. But you believe that I believe?"

"I wholeheartedly believe that you definitely believe this."

"Then that's a good start. What are some of your questions?"

"Ok, first of all. The lives, they span a variety of worlds, realms, dimensions and universes I take it?"

"As a matter of fact, yes. Time is the only constant connecting the lives. Time for the most part seems to always only move forward. I do not believe I have ever traveled backwards or forwards. I do think I've been in bent-time many times, however."

"Now what's bent-time?"

Commander Bryant motioned to me to stop the tape.

"Bent-time?" Commander Bryant asked clearing his throat.

"Yes, sir."

"I thought this was a hoax theory thought up by that tight sort, Cheddar."

"You mean, Chowder, Sir." The Deputy standing at attention corrected Commander Bryant.

"Thank you, sir," Commander Bryant said not without a hint of irritation scrapping against his throat.

"Yes, it was a hoax theory, Commander. However, the concept was very plausible and according to Vladimir, there are worlds where bent time stands as universal laws."

"This is what interested me for the past few years about this 'entity.' The worlds that it's seen, and to remember them all, it baffles me. It also makes me wonder what my own reality is about. What is its meaning?"

"I understand very well what you mean, Commander," I rose from the desk and walked toward a glass decanter tucked away in the back corner of the office. "Would you like a drink?"

"Yes, thank you."

I poured whiskey from the decanter into two glasses.

"Sorry I don't have any ice," I said handing three fingers filled of liquor to Commander Bryant.

"This is great, thank you," he responded raising his glass in cheers.

This whiskey relaxed our bellies and the tension took its time evaporating from the room. The Deputy by the door continued to stand at attention.

"Ever since I met, Vladimir," I started. "I have come to do a great deal of existential and spiritual thinking the likes of which I had never done before. The very existence of an entity fully and totally aware of itself from moment to moment, lifetime after lifetime, is simply baffling. The idea itself has broken my psyche at least 3 or 4 times. It begs the question, what does this all mean? What are we even doing?"

"Yes, that's the same question I've been asking myself ever since I started watching Vladimir's memories."

"Wait, what?"

"Right. Dr. Cane, as I said. I am conducting an investigation of the utmost importance to national security and your invaluable assistance isn't just required but necessary. From what you say, and the interest you yourself have taken in the 'entity' previously known as Vladimir Fortune, I believe together we will be able to put this puzzle together."

And with that, I joined the team self-tasked to learn about, understand, hunt down and capture the 'entity.'

While Commander Bryant was losing himself into the memory playback of Vladimir Fortune, provided by the Doctor's machine, Niki Brown and her husband Alain Machado were still fighting. Handling defeat in a destructive manner after Vladimir Fortune's bloody and untimely death, the married couple were on the verge of collapse. Niki's unauthorized roll in the hay with our story's main person of interest, Vladimir Fortune, has caused deviation within the plan. Together they fell into the deepest depths of despair that anyone could dig up. When we return to them, it has been two years since they lost Vladimir Fortune's location and caused one of the most embarrassing failed missions of the Company Security Division's long outstandingly great history.

Alain was fired for incompetence and Niki was reassigned to protective detail in Company 1. Adding insult to injury, she was assigned to protect the Tungalao ambassador Justine Bryant, Commander Bryant's wife.

Niki Brown had no problem with Justine Bryant. In fact, as far as women went, Niki considered Justine to be admirable and almost a role model. But she fucked Justine's husband, so there was no reconciliation between the two women. The tribunal ordered the reassignment and no one questioned the Tribunal. A flaw in the programming of citizens living in the United Companies of America. But we'll get to that soon.

The two women handled the reassignment with poise and strength, as women naturally do. Days were filled with schedules and perimeter sweeps. Holding for positioning, surveillance and body checks. Nights were spent in drunken sorrow for the both of them. Separately they shared the same suffering in connected hotel suites. The sobs of the other were as comforting as wool blankets for privileged children.

As Niki tried her best to deal with the blow, fate and her failure had cost her. Her husband, Alain, had lost himself in drink. There was an assortment of liquors that surrounded Alain when we see him again. Slumped over onto the black coach in his and his wife's 2 bedroom flat. The clothes he wore had been strapped to him for the past week and he smelled of alcohol and feces. Alain took the downfall following Vlad's violent death horribly. He was dead by the time Niki was removed from Justine Bryant's security detail, for publicly punching her in the face and subsequently breaking her nose.

All this happened, as Commander Bryant watched playbacks of Vladimir Fortune's memories. Ignoring everything, his position of Commander was lifetime. So, he needn't worry, and after all, he was engrossed in research.

Engrossed he was. When the two of us linked, he introduced me to the machine; thus, began for me the prime point for my reason of living. Before that, however, let us go back to the tapes.

**Tape 1 continued:**

"This is Dr. Leon Cane, testing one-two. Ok, welcome back. Sorry about that, I had a bit of an emergency. Thanks for letting me take an hour break between our sessions."

"Is everything alright?" A young Vladimir can be heard asking from the tape playback.

"Yea, everything's fine. Well, not fine really. My wife's mother passed away earlier this morning."

"I'm sorry to hear that."

"Thanks. She's heading to Company 22, where my wife's from."

"Company 22 is nice. A lot of land."

"A whole lot of land. Anyway, she's handling it better than I would. So..."

"You're just trying to do your best?"

"Right. Alright then, where were we?"

"Past lives."

"Yes, you remember quite a few of them."

"I do. My memories are starting to blend together though. My dreams too, it's beginning to become harder and harder to distinguish between the two."

"Your dreams and memories you mean?"

"Yea, and my memories of dreams."

"How vivid are your memories from past lives?"

"Vivid. Sometimes the memories, or what I think is a memory anyway, are in my mind with such clarity that I question whether or not this is actually reality."

"That's why you're in here."

"No. I'm in here because of the nightmares."

"What nightmares?"

"Over the last year or so. When I sleep, I fall into a different world. It's a world that I've never been in before. The sky is forever glowing orange from the flames stretching across the roads. As far as the eye can see, highways upon highways of crisscrossing roads blazing fire."

"What do you know about this world?"

"Nothing. I've only found myself there. I know it's a real place though."

"Not just a dream?"

"No, this place is real and I'm being pulled there."

"Do you ever walk around this nightmare world?"

"Never. I can never move. I try not to sleep as much because I'm so petrified of this place. I wish I could describe the feeling to you, Dr. Cane, of being in this awful world. The heat of the fire and the smell of sulfur in the air, it's always too much to bear."

"Do you ever see anything else beside the highway of roads?"

"Nope. Just the roads on fire."

"Are all of the roads always empty?"

A long silence in the tape startled Commander Bryant into thinking the playback machine had broken. I reassured him with a gentle wave that everything was fine. He comforted and continued to listen.

"Not every time."

"Sometimes there's someone on one of the roads?"

"Yea, not all the time though. It's very rare that you see him."

"See who?"

"The Crimson Knight."

"The Crimson Knight?"

"I don't know if that's what it's called. That's what I call it. I just got through reading the 'Dark Tower' series, there was a Crimson something in there. So, I just started calling it the Crimson Knight."

"What does it look like?"

"A giant knight succumbed in black atop an equally massive horse."

"What does it do?"

"Seems to just stalk the burning highways. It's always far away and I always wake myself up after a certain amount of time after being in the hellish world."

"How often do you have this nightmare, Vladimir?"

"At first it was just once in a while. But it's becoming more and more frequent. Kinda becoming something of an obsession when I'm awake too."

"Is there something about it that fascinates you?"

"I just don't know where the hell it is? I've done a lot of research trying to figure it out. But I can't just tell anyone because they'll think I'm crazy."

"Do you have anyone that you're close to that you are able to share things with? Remember your past lives for example?"

"There's a few people. Not very many though. I tell everyone I meet about remembering my past lives. Most people tend to write it off that I'm just being a dick or trying to be funny. It's very rare when someone will actually take interest."

"So, you remembering your past lives isn't something that's a secret or anything?"

"Heaven's no. I do have secrets from those past lives but that's not the same thing."

"No, I don't suppose it is. Have you told anyone else ever about the nightmare, or the Crimson Knight?"

"I've told my teacher about that."

"Your teacher?"

"Yes, Sifu Ping."

"And who is Sifu Ping?"

"Sifu Ping was my master from a previous life whom I fused with when he died."

"You fused with your master when he died?"

"Yes, and now he lives on inside of my mind. My master is the one that has helped me organize the memories of all my past lives."

"Can he not help you deal with these nightmares?"

"My master, Sifu Ping, unfortunately is dying. He's very old. Fusing was just so that I could continue to advance. I'm a rather slow-witted learner I'm afraid."

"I'm so lost right now, Vladimir."

"Vlad's ok."

"Alright, Vlad. Let's just go back a little bit, can we?"

"Sure, no problem."

"Ok. Now, putting aside the nightmare-blazing-fire-highway, with the Crimson Knight galloping around, for just a moment. Let's return to this idea that you can remember your past lives.'

"Yes."

"You say that time is the only constant in your experience when it comes to each life you've lived over the last, how many did you say it's been?"

"I think I'm on 18 now. The count is more of a guesstimated thing. Especially for the lives that were in different realms on a different world then this one."

"So, you're saying that you've lived on different planets?"

"Even different universes, I think."

"But I could say that we all do that naturally. Depending upon my belief, what you're talking about can be happening to each one of us moment after moment, lifetimes and lifetimes wrapped in each instant."

"Yes, that's true. I never said that's what makes me special. I never said I was special. But the reason that I'm sitting here talking to you is because I can remember all of that stuff that's going on for each one of us naturally as a law of life."

"That's the part that seems, unnatural."

"Precisely."

"And then you tuck in the Crimson Knight and some guy named Sifu Ping living on inside of your mind."

"And there you have the ingredients to make a madman cocktail. Best taken stirred, not shaken."

"I guess I'm about to try one of those soon enough. Have you ever gone through Thought Therapy before?"

"No, this is my first time."

"Ok, great. Well, what do you know about it?"

"I know that you take a lot of drugs, hook up to a virtual reality simulator and then together we dive into my head."

"That's essentially about right. Are you ready for the drug taking portion?"

"Half the reason I'm here, doc."

"Mr. Fortune, I'd request that you not joke in this manner and take the process of Thought Therapy seriously."

"My apologies, Dr. Cane. I do take this incredibly seriously. If I'm going to keep remembering these lives I'd like to not be traumatized while I do."

"Yes, I can understand that desire very well, Vladimir. Ok, let's get started. I'm going to first need you to take these two orange pills and then in exactly 7 minutes you're going to take these two purple pills."

"And what are these exactly?"

"The orange pills will help you relax and fall into an almost dreamlike state, while staying awake. The purple ones will take away any anxiety that will most certainly arise during our session. Time is going to be felt at an alarmingly different rate and the experience oftentimes is over-jarring for many. We have these ingested as a precaution."

"Ok, I trust you doc."

"Well I'm happy to hear that, Mr. Fortune. While we wait for the 7 minutes to pass, let's get you hooked up to the simulator."

"I have to tell you, I'm awfully nervous all of a sudden doc."

"That's perfectly natural. Just wait until the pills kick in. Your 7 minutes are up. Time for the purple ones now. That's good. Now, are you comfortable?"

"As comfortable as I can be, considered I'm in a dentist chair."

"Well it's not as bad as the dentist and you're about to feel a whole lot more relaxed once those pills take full effect. Now, I just want you to lie back and let your head rest on the back of the cushion just like that. That's good. Now, what I'm going to do next is attach an adhesive to your temples on both sides of your head. Attached to the adhesive are electrodes that we'll use to monitor your brain. And I'm going to put this one right here on your finger to monitor your heart. Alright that's good. How do you feel, Vladimir?"

"More comfortable."

"I believe the pills are beginning to work their magic."

"So, how long before we go into my head?"

"There are a few things we will need to go over first before we can get to all of the fun and games. It's important that you understand that everything we are about to see is coming from your mind. The world and possibly worlds we transverse are all apart of you. Everything in this world will recognize you and assist you. I will only be allowed to exist inside of your mind together with you, so long as you allow me to do so. This is why it's of the utmost importance that you do not forget the world we are in is coming from your mind. Do you understand this?"

"Don't forget we are in my mind. Check."

"Ok, good. If I find that you have lost control of this understanding, I will pull us out and our session will have to end for the day."

"Does this happen a lot?"

"People forgetting that what they're seeing is coming from their own minds?"

"Yea."

"Yep, all the time. It's actually quite dangerous. That's why you signed all those waivers before even stepping foot into my office. Thought Therapy is still a risqué practice. The Tribunal approved of its use, however, the superstition surrounding it and the fact that there are drugs involved still makes people very uneasy."

"I'm perfectly alright with the drug use. What'd you think it's going to look like in there, Doc?"

"Honestly, I have no clue. I'm excited to find out. Cautious, but very excited. I do think we should be ready for the possibility of a couple different versions of you existing in whatever worlds we are about to walk into, living within your mind. I'm almost certain there's going to be trauma from past lives which is going to be fascinating to observe. I don't know what the hell we're going to see. But I think we should get started."


**TAPE #1** ended and I sat and stared at Commander Bryant for some time, waiting for his words to come out.

He removed a cigar from the breast pocket of his uniform. He hadn't given any indication of the cigar's existence nor had he the demeanor of a smoker, quickly reminding me that one never knew what was lurking inside of another's brain. No matter how many therapy sessions, I was always surprised by what I discovered inside another's mind.

"The therapy sessions themselves. Do you have any recordings of these? Is it even possible to record and play it back, Dr. Cane?"

"No, it's not," I answered the Commander. "We have to rely solely on the recorded logs I make after each session ends."

"You have those?"

"I do."

"Good," Commander Bryant said rising abruptly. "This has been very helpful. I won't take up any more of your time. I've got meetings and I'm sure you've got appointments."

Commander Bryant and I shook hands and he took his leave ending the start of a colleagueship that centered on the mysterious enigma that existed in Vladimir Fortune.

I'm not very sure that Commander Bryant had much of an idea of what he was doing. I knew from our first meeting he had taken an obsessive interest in the entity that used to be Vladimir Fortune. But I wasn't sure if he was trying to capture the entity or if he had just become trapped within the story he had been watching unfold in the fragments of Vladimir's broken and distorted memories of past lives. I knew one thing though, I wanted to see the playback video of those memories that had stolen the purpose of Commander Bryant's existence.

It didn't take long for me to become addicted. And then the two of us began to spend entire days and weeks watching playback after playback. I'm not exactly sure when we decided to start trying to make sense out of it and piece it together chronologically. Once we did, though, that's when the Tribunal's reason for taking such a great interest in the case of Vladimir Fortune began to clearly illuminate.

◆  ◆  ◆

When I was younger, I had an uncanny fear that my mother would die in a car accident during a terrible thunderstorm. Whenever I would hear a clap of thunder, the fear would arise no matter if my mother was beside me or not. In this I was inconsolable. As time moved along, my parents had another boy and my younger brother came into the world. He was a fiery kid but we got along and I was happy to not be alone anymore.

As he grew older and began to venture out on his own in the world, I applied my fear of my mother dying a gruesome death to him. How my imagination would create such horrific ways of meeting an ill-fated end.

I had the great fortune of going abroad and escaping the United Companies of America for a few years after becoming 18 years of age and successfully completing the Primary classes of K-12. Secondary education was optional and rather unattainable for most of us living in the UCA, so, there was no reason to try. It's interesting how easily one can forget that the pursuit of education is the most important of them all. Even easier to forget if such a concept was never taught.

My parents did their utmost to protect me and I wholeheartedly know they gave magnificent efforts towards educating me, to the best of their abilities. However, their best was not good enough and when I won the chance to study abroad after submitting an essay on the thought pattern of Serial Killers, I jumped at the opportunity.

Being interested in serial killers was not unusual when I was 17, as there was a serial killer on the loose who the media coined to calling, The Cat Clown.

The Cat Clown would dress up in a clown suit and paint his face like a clown, but for some reason, he would put whiskers on his face as well. Lots of whiskers, it was later discovered when he was finally gunned down in a climatic shootout with police after an unsuccessful attempt of abduction. The Cat Clown was in reality the son of Fernando Gordon, inventor of the implants every citizen in the UC of A are required, by law mind you, to have injected into their heads from the back of the ears. At birth they do this to us, and only us. No other country has authorized the experimental communications device to be implanted into humans. None accept the country that created Fernando Gordon, the United Companies of America.

There was a time when, before I was born, the country stood firm and strong. Once the hate disunited us all into uncountable categories of fake news, the lands economy tanked. Heavily disrupting the equilibrium of what used to be called the United States of America, was holding us together. Desperation called for an immediate fix to the fall of the American Empire. The Grape family stepped in and introduced the companies that would become the owners of all of the 50 states of what America had so long boasted about, being united.

It was no secret that Fernando Gordon was a hack inventor that got ahold of a cutting-edge technology, in almost certainly immoral ways, and threw his mother's life savings into creating a prototype. The prototype took the interest of the Tribunal, that most secret of organizations, which emerged conveniently around the same time as the 50 states were sold to the highest bidders. That's all it took really.

Literally in the blink of an eye, implants were as common as Steve Jobs iPhone in that long-ago time before the great crumble of earth's ecosystem. Seeming to have more money than God, Fernando Gordon went about becoming infamous for drugs, sex, and bad radio music. It came as no surprise that his son, Casper Van Dyke Gordon, would fall into some questionable ways. Serial Killer did raise a few eyebrows, thus making it the hot topic in all forums of media discussion. It wasn't weird that I wrote an essay on serial killers at the time.

What did capture the interest of the judges was my ability to project analysis of psychotic behavior in a way that specialist had never seen before. I don't at all know what exactly made me write what I did, to me it all came out very naturally. What I wrote was what I thought and I thought everyone thought the same way as I did, at the time. It didn't take very long to learn that this was not the case. In fact, no one thought the way I did.

At that moment though when I won that essay contest and got to travel to China, there wasn't much that I understood about what was happening in my life.

I guess the United Companies of America had existed for at least 2 generations before I came along. I can't quite recall but I do think I remember my grandmother talking about life in the "good ol' U.S. of A." From what I recall it wasn't that great by then, but I guess that's why it came to an end. The first thing I learned when I got off the Solar Jet in China was that the UCA wasn't that great either.

I would learn later the irony of standing in China and thinking to myself, this is what freedom felt like. But it was freer than I had ever hoped to believe, or even known to exist. The one flaw, if you could call it such a thing, was that other countries could block its usage in their borders. Given that it was a telecommunications device that is exactly what the UN did. A block was introduced and the implant that Fernando Gordon had invented was rendered useless the moment the host entered. Every country unanimously accepted the defense against the UCA's spy implant, as it is known outside of the country.

I also quickly learned that all of the information we were taught in Primary school about the world beyond our own borders, was false.

I think more than anything, experiencing life outside of the UCA was why it didn't take much for me to believe Vladimir when he told me that he could remember his past lives. I definitely didn't need much convincing once we dove into his Though Therapy Sessions and I actually got to see inside of his mind. Let me tell ya, I'd had a good number of clients before Vlad. And a great number of them were very crazy to some degree. One or two had absolutely killed someone, I was sure of it. So, I saw a lot of fucked up things. But what I saw when I went into Vladimir Fortunes mind, let me tell you, would scare the shit outta Jesus.

The program that I had entered because I won the essay contest was a direct route to becoming a Thought Therapist. So, with no real ambition coupled with my parents believing that I would make lots of money and become respectable, I went ahead and worked to get my degree in Psychology.

My brother and I kept in touch while I was away studying and tried our best to see each other whenever we could. What no one in the family knew when I went away to China to begin the road toward becoming a Thought Therapist, was that for the next ten years I was to do what I was told. In a lot of ways, my cruel tutelage was very much like being in the military. Which makes a lot of sense to a degree because the majority of graduates went on to assist cadets during basic, and primarily specialized in assisting those in combat zones.

Once returning from China and acclimating myself back to the "good ol' U.C. of A." I entered into my profession of thought therapy as an apprentice. It was during these years that I began to walk inside of other people's minds. This was an experience to say the least. It's not as difficult of an experience as one would believe to be, very easy to adjust to. I excelled as a quick study and in the blink of an eye later, in my memory, I was seeing patients as a thought therapist.

In the beginning of my adventures in thought therapy, I hadn't a clue how the practice could be effective in the multifaceted world we lived in. There wasn't a single amount of hope I felt I could instill into the individuals boldly stepping foot into the office, allowing themselves to be subjected to drugs, virtual reality and a mind guide, that's me, to walk them through it all.

When I entered Vladimir Fortune's mind, Sonata No. 3 in F Minor by Vladimir Horowitz was playing in my ears. The soft twinkle of the keys reacting to the masterful maestro's elegant fingers washed a sense of drama over the scene. In all my years as a thought therapist, I had never before witnessed such beauty as displayed in the mind of Vlad. The memories of past lives, the entity that was Vladimir had lived reflecting the vast landscape of time. A clash of dimensions, worlds and universes collided creating a landscape of unparalleled view. My breath was literally taken away from all that I saw.

As we began to transverse the nooks and crannies of Vlad's mind, we came to an endless set of stairs. I say endless because I could not see the bottom of where they ended. With no way to the left or right of us to go, we had entered into the hollow of a mountain blocking the path we were being directed to walk upon. Here's a fun fact that only a thought therapist would know, the worlds of creation inside of our minds almost always have a path laid out to be followed that will lead one to whatever it is that they are trying their best to find, inside of their minds. These little hints at bringing ourselves to our, hearts essentially, is at the core of living. A lasting promise of the inevitable revolution within. So down the steps we went.

I relayed this to Commander Bryant as we eat dinner at Grapola immediately following that first meeting in my office.

"Let's hold off on all that for a moment. I need to know some more details about what Vladimir shared with you," Commander Bryant said after polishing off a steak and mashed potato combo plate.

"You heard the full tape," I responded sipping on the pint of beer I had been nursing for over an hour.

"You should just finish that thing," Commander Bryant said to me, reading my mind.

I did as suggested and repeated my previous statement. "You heard the full tape."

"You had other sessions," he quickly retorted.

"Yes, that is true."

"Then, it's those that I'm talking about." He looked at me with fire in his eyes. It was then I began to see the personal stake he had in Vladimir Fortune. Or was it the entity? I didn't know. But the feeling of that intensity told me I had no reason to try and ascertain for myself what it was he wanted with the man that could remember his past lives.

I gave him one of the puzzled looks you give when trying to bluff at the poker table and not having practiced at it in the mirror at home enough. He didn't fall for my bluff.

"I can always just confiscate them, Doctor Cane. You seem like an ok enough guy and I believe that together we can uncover quite a few more layers towards understanding whatever this entity is."

The thing that had been irking me since meeting Commander Bryant, gnawed its way out of the cage I held it in.

"Why, are you so confident there's anything different about this human being, besides that it can remember past lives? That doesn't mean there's some secret locked away in the memories of Vladimir Fortune. We all have past lives and we all live them in different worlds. Some of us can just remember more than others. Vlad could just remember an extraordinary amount more than probably anyone ever living has before."

"Mr. Chase, the piano player, remembered as many lives as Vlad. As far as we know that is."

I looked at him dumbfounded. Who on earth was Mr. Chase, the piano player? And I'm not embarrassed to admit it, but I realized at precisely that moment that Commander Bryant could reduce my life to beneath zero before we finished the dinner we were eating. This thought humbled and sobered me. I knocked back the 2$^{nd}$ beer that had arrived a few minutes prior and then asked the question aloud. "Who is Mr. Chase, the piano player?"

As expected, almost choreographically so, Commander Bryant smiled wider for the first time than I had ever seen him do before. We had only just met, technically, but he had provided me with significantly acceptable and polite minor stretches of his lips and checks; on his face I should add just for clarification.

"There's a lot that we can help each other with, Dr. Cane," Commander Bryant said waving the server over for our tab. He had his shadow, who never seemed to be beyond the eyesight of the Commander. We gathered our coats and walked outside. The acid rains had returned and we each tapped our implants for the layer of protection we so desperately needed if we were to walk in the acid rainstorm just starting up.

Commander Bryant motioned me into the car that pulled up to the curb just as we arrived to it. The shadow amazingly was driving. He ran to the curb side back doors and opened them for us, I'm sure more for Commander Bryant than me. Not feeling the urge to walk in acid rain if I didn't have to, I climbed into the back seat.

The door slammed and off we went.

"I'd like us to enter a partnership," Commander Bryant said to me after letting some time pass in the backseat. The city was boisterous and citizens alike were out and about, in spite of the acid rainstorm. Such scenes made the implants seem more like gifts than devices of control. Why not both? I thought to myself as I saw two lovers running hand-in-hand across the street.

"Did you hear me?" Commander Bryant politely asked.

I had heard him just fine, of course. But given his full control of the situation. Any semblance of control I could snatch I was willing to take. "I'm sorry, what did you say?" I asked feigning the act of zoning out.

He threw on that smile I came to love so much. It was chilling how the recognition that he could have me erased at any moment, enthralled me so.

"I'd like us to enter a partnership. There are certain things that I cannot divulge to you. However, I am in a position to compensate you greatly for your assistance. And as I said, it would be a partnership. So, you would be promoted to the rank equal to my own. I'd see to this personally. Let me tell you, Dr. Cane, my rank holds perks only a handful of citizens get to enjoy."

"I've heard about you, Commander Bryant."

"That does not surprise me. You did very good playing aloof."

"I make a living out of taking drugs and going into other people's minds. You pick up a lot of things along the way in a profession like mine."

"I imagine so. Your study of thought therapy is another intriguing element and reason why I wish to enter into a partnership with you."

"I know about you Tribunal people's partnerships."

"I am not a member of the Tribunal, Dr. Cane."

"Yea, but you work for them."

"As a Commander in the Company Security Division, yes I do serve the Tribunal. As we all do."

"We all do not serve the Tribunal," I snapped surprising even myself.

That awfully seductive smile stretched across Commander Bryant's face again. "Dr. Cane," he said slow and deliberately. You of all people are fully aware of the position every citizen of the United Companies of America is in at this current moment. There is no one, living in this land of ours that is not a servant to the Tribunal. There is a greater control that you are not aware of, and it is for this reason that I am requesting a partnership with you."

"I can't serve the Tribunal directly, sir."

"Dr. Cane," Commander Bryant replied. "You're not looking at this with the proper lens on. There are things at work here that are beyond what is taught in your books."

"Well, Commander, if you want me to enter into a partnership with you then you're going to have to tell me about those things."

That smile never left his face as I stared at him, long and hard. I tried to leverage the tiniest of gains I had achieved. My bluff paid off this time.

"You make a very good point, Dr. Cane. What would you like to know?"

Stunned that my ploy was successful, I sat with my mouth agape. I had no idea of what to say. My mind was racing. Then, suddenly a question formed in my brain, but I held on to it in hesitation. I looked around the car we had entered and had been riding in. The leather upholstery that I was sure I had taken notice of when I first stepped into the car, became apparent to me just then. I looked around the backseat and took notice of the bar sitting near our ankles.

I had heard the clinking glasses throughout the ride to that point but had taken no notice of the strangeness of it. Everything was already so strange.

"Mind if I have a drink," I asked Commander Bryant stalling for time.

"Please go right ahead," he said with that damn sexy smile that cut straight through to let me know he was still in control. I made for the chalice of brown liquid and poured myself a drink.

"Can I get you one?" I asked holding an empty glass over my left shoulder toward him.

"Yea, sure why not. I have a feeling you're about to ask me something I may have trouble answering."

I poured him a drink. Sitting in the bench-seats with the driver to my back and staring at Commander Bryant with the road disappearing in the distance behind him, for the first time I took notice of the scar that was just above his right eyelid. It was an insignificant keloid of a thing and I'm not sure why it grasped my attention. It did though.

Commander Bryant paid me no attention and enjoyed his glass of whiskey. It was his and it was expensive. I shook my head of the image of the scar above his right eyelid and returned to the question that had popped into my head.

"Tell me about the Tribunal," I asked.

"Not the most original, but I supposed expected of questions. Well, what do you know of the Tribunal?" Commander Bryant asked deflecting.

"I know as much as the next citizen does, which isn't a whole lot."

"And what is that, for context sake, so I know where to begin from."

"How much do you know?"

"Almost everything, Dr. Cane. I know almost everything there is to know about the Tribunal. My father was one of its founding members. I am what you could call, Royalty in these United Companies of America."

Once he said that I could see the royalty wafting off of him. It was always there; I just didn't have a name for it. This explained his smile. It was the white-washed smile of privilege that reached godly proportions following the selling of the 50 states. As a black guy, I knew this aura well.

"As time is short, and as fun as this is, I'll move us along and tell you about the Tribunal. When the Grape family auctioned off what used to be the 50 states, a group of wealthy men and women from scatters of the world came together and formed an alliance. The sole purpose of this alliance was to ensure that the citizens passively accept and adhere to the laws and regulations as set forth by the group. They became known as the Tribunal following the Great Bit Coin Scam. The companies that purchased each state had no interest in governing anything. The members that formed the Tribunal, however, had a great interest in it. It was the need of ensuring that millions of citizens were able to transition into the new order of things without much resistance."

"This is when the Tribunal purchased the implant from the inventor and somehow made it mandatory for every citizen to have it injected."

"Yes, that's correct. It's not as far off as you may think though, Dr. Cane. When the country fell because of the president's dirty misdeeds, everyone could feel the powder keg about to explode."

The noun powder keg had a fascinating reaction on me at that particular moment. When Commander Bryant said it, the image of an exploding raisin popped into my head. There suddenly, while riding in Commander Bryant's luxury limo, I was thinking of exploding raisins gushing purple juice all over the screen of my mind's vision. This thought dissipated to very little and all that consisted in my reality was exploding raisins. The whole thing was quite jarring and I did my best to rid it out of my thoughts. There was little that could be done, though.

"This would be why the implants were necessary," Commander Bryant said breaking me from whatever the hell had been happening. He had been talking the entire time I was visualizing exploding raisins, but I missed all of what he said. I made for the minibar at our ankles and tried to cover up my confusion with thirst. Downing my drink didn't help I'm sure but the entire scene, to be honest, was starting to stress me the fuck out.

Commander Bryant continued on.

"After the implants were introduced it didn't take long for every citizen to have one. It was the natural progression following the smartphone becoming obsolete. In the beginning there was of course a great push back from citizens not wanting to fall into the trap of control by a select group of 'chosen' powerful people. The lasting impression on everyone at that point in the country, however, was one of utter numbness. The last president being hauled off to jail following the sale off all 50 states to Iran, China and Russia was enough to send the citizens of what was once the United States of America into a frenzied pace of panic and turmoil."

The luxury sedan limo came to a sudden halt and I realized we were before the CSD headquarters. The 100-storied building stretched beyond the clouds it seemed. The acid rainstorm had abated and the sky was beginning to clear. The sun tried its best to make appearances through the transparent dome protecting us all.

"I'm afraid we'll have to pause here. I'd like you to follow me upstairs to my office, Dr. Cane," Commander Bryant said. Deputy Shadow opened the door and I got out after the Commander. The outside wasn't fresh, but it never is. Somehow the stale stench of the city had grown on me. I embraced its odor as if it was coming off of an old relative that decided never to leave the house after visiting, as I've heard relatives often do with friends. My parents seldom left their Company and my brother wasn't a nuisance such as that.

The ding of the elevator cleared my mind completely of the thoughts that had been racing furiously toward the finish line. Of what, I had no idea of. We boarded the elevator car and made our way upwards toward the 100th floor. The wall opposite of the sliding doors was made of glass and had been positioned on the very edge of the building, giving the occupant of the elevator a superb view of the ever-evolving city. There was no way to tell that at that very moment we were embarking on a path that would lead us both to prison.

When the metallic doors slid open, Deputy Shadow got out first and held them open for Commander Bryant. I'm sure I was just an innocent bystander to his courtesy. I followed behind the two of them, the Commander in front with that damn smile I'm sure smacked across his face, leading the way.

His office was located at the very end of the floor, the 100th level was just one long hallway, windows for every wall, ceiling and floor. The floor windows were by far the most interesting. One could see below, but the floor under only saw a black glass ceiling. I'll have to admit it was fun watching people scuttle about around their cubicles and navigate the rat race of corporate world.

"Don't stare too long, Doctor," Commander Bryant said, holding the door into his office for me.

I walked inside and had my breath immediately taken away. As far as offices went, Commander Bryant's was by far the best that I'd ever seen. The thing that caught my attention was the cheap furry white throw rug near the fireplace. The Commander caught my eye and stretched that obnoxious smile even wider.

Nodding his head quickly in the direction of the fluffy white throw rug I was admiring so hard, Commander Bryant said, "shall we sit by the fire and continue our conversation?"

This seemed like the best course of action, so I complied. Quite delighted to be closer to the cheap furry white throw rug. Snuggling up on it, close but not too close to the fireplace, I got ready to hear the rest of what Commander Bryant had to tell me about the Tribunal.

He seemed reluctant to begin, so I asked if he had anymore whiskey. As I assumed correctly, he had a never-ending supply of the brown liquid. Every single type, as well. As the liquid drifted down our throats and into our bellies, the Commander's tongue loosened.

"Where the Tribunal got their power, is the source of the mystery that surrounds them," Commander Bryant said abruptly after we had been talking on whom was the best James Bond. My vote was Idris Elba.

"What do you mean?" I asked him finally intrigued that the conversation had returned to the important matter at hand.

"The Tribunal's power!" Commander Bryant forcefully said, breaking character for just a second. "It comes from the Fire Demon."

It was at this point that I was sure the Commander had lost his mind. I glanced at the Deputy that shadowed him always and raised an eyebrow. His training did not betray him and he shot back at me the same concrete look. With no choice, I asked the question.

"What is the Fire Demon?"

Boy did he have an answer for me.

"The Fire Demon," Commander Bryant (as if you didn't know) began. "It is a demon that has existed longer than time has been recorded as we know it. I'm not even sure how that's possible, but it is. This thing has been around for a very long time."

"What is it?" I asked, annoyingly I'm sure.

"A demon," he answered dryly with that damn grin on his face again.

"Yes, I'd figured as much, Commander," I responded not making any types of effort to disguise my irritation. "What kind of demon?"

"A fire demon," he said with again that damn smile searing into me, making me more and more pissed off.

"Ok, how does the Tribunal get their power from this 'fire demon'?"

"Through human sacrifice, of course. Blood, Doctor Cane. The fire demon that the Tribunal has attached themselves to in order to obtain power, demands copious amounts of blood."

"And we citizens provide that blood?"

"Yes, Doctor Cane. That is the crux of it all, I'm afraid. And now, because of Vladimir Fortune's memories, that fire demon is demanding something it never has before." Commander Bryant finished leaning back into the armchair he was resting in which sat on top of the cheap furry white throw rug. I observed the Commander and for the first time noticed a new strange aspect I thought never existed within such a man.

.Fear.

# Chapter Four:

## Bear-Wolf's and Other Memories of Commander Bryant

From that point onward, the Commander and I spent a great deal of time together. He and I got to know one another fairly well. Also, I learned of the Commanders strict upbringing by his father, the very famous Admiral Granite.

"You know, the old man was a son of a bitch," Commander Bryant would say to me whenever we took a break from viewing Vlad's memories on the playback machine. "I never hated him. But I never fully liked him either."

"I think that's usual with most sons and their fathers. I'm not sure it's possible to fully like one's father at all. Even if the father does a good enough job, there is so much emotional baggage that comes from growing up in any kind of environment nurturing or otherwise," I responded automatically falling into my practiced doctor's spiel.

"Yea, having a famous father didn't help all that much either. Because of his rank and the fame, I didn't see him so much after I reached a certain age. In the beginning though, we did a lot of stuff together."

"Like what?"

"By far my favorite thing to do together with my dad was our hunting trips beyond the rim."

I looked at the Commander startled at what he just said. "Your father would take you beyond the rim?"

The commander attached that irritating smile onto his lips and nodded his head yes.

"Of course my father took me beyond the rim. A few times a year he would take me into the forest and we hunted the different beasts that live there."

I shook my head in disbelief. "That's insane. There are all kinds of beasts in the forest."

That damn confident smile splashed even wider across his face. "Oh yes, you are correct. The different rejects of the experimentation period following the collapse of the USA and just before the UCA was formed, were cast to the forest once the rim was built. There was great lawlessness when the States were announced as sold to the various countries, which were historically known to be dictatorial. That is when the Tribunal stepped in, built the rim around the country and saved the citizens from destroying themselves."

"Is that how you see it," I asked feeling the rebel in me spark up.

"Now I'm not getting political, but it is pretty factual that if someone hadn't stepped in and united the citizens, the different factions that had begun to break off would've brought about a direct end to any semblance of civility in this country."

"So, we handed over our freedom!?" I spat back beyond my control two cease the urge. I wasn't even sure I believed in the words coming out of my mouth. Pulled forth from the anger I had held so calmly deep down in my belly, hoping it would all one day just go away. As I spoke I knew, however, that those words were from my heart.

"No, we didn't hand over our freedom. We've never had our freedom to hand over in the first place. But what we did have we didn't need to lose. And for that reason, the Tribunal stepping in and bringing a status quo back into the countries' reality was the right move to make; as far as survival was concerned."

I shook my head in disgust. But there were other pressing matters at hand, I thought as I cringed at the Commander's smile. "Moving away from all of that for just a minute. How does all of this have anything to do with the Tribunal getting their power from a Fire Demon?"

Just then the Shadow emerged from the shadows and ran over and whispered something into the Commander's ear. He nodded a few times never taking his eyes off of mine. His smile was nowhere to be seen. Commander Bryant said something I couldn't hear after the Deputy finished relaying the message and ran out of the office with a look upon his face I hadn't seen up until that moment.

"Is everything ok?" I asked rising from the furry white throw rug. Commander Bryant stood,

"Yes, everything's fine," he said standing from the chair he had been so comfortably sitting in. "I will have to ask you to remain here for a bit, however, there has been a security breach in the building and we are on lockdown."

"What kind of security breach?"

"The dangerous kind, I'm afraid. As we speak, the lobby of this building is being secured by a tactical unit and the floors will be swept one-by-one until every inch has been cleared safe. It's standard operating procedure, there's nothing that can be done about it. Would you like another glass?" he asked walking toward the chalice.

Seeing as I had no reason not to drink, as if I ever need a reason to drink, I shrugged my shoulders and said yes to another glass.

"Personally, I'm glad that you're here. I'm usually alone when these things happen and honestly it gets pretty depressing up here when you're by yourself."

"Being trapped doesn't help at all, I can imagine."

"No, being trapped is not fun. But this isn't trapped, really."

"No, I suppose you're right. This is more of an inconvenient occurrence."

"You have a nice way with words, Doctor Cane."

"I was instructed by the very best," Commander Bryant said. "Studied long and hard to become the man that stands here before you today."

"And just who is this man that they call, Doctor Cane?"

"Well," I started in non-hesitation. I had been waiting my entire adult life for someone to ask this question. "Doctor Cane is not a patient man. Which is something of a contradiction being that one of the primary requirements of my profession is patience. Yet, when it comes to my work, I can endure whatever I must."

"Are you just that passionate about what you do?" Commander Bryant asked becoming enthralled by what I was saying. I wasn't quite sure what I was saying as the alcohol had begun to take full effect.

"Yes, I guess I would say that I am incredibly passionate about thought therapy."

"What exactly is the draw that pulls you into this particular field? You have to admit that it is a strange field of study," Commander Bryant said knocking back glass numbered…, or rather of the forgotten count.

"It's one of the most bizarre fields of study," I said darting my hands outward. The small amount of liquid I still had in my glass sloshed out and fell towards the furry white throw rug. I grimaced my face and braced to feel the impact of my mistake.

"Don't worry about it," he said and then asked. "Do you want another?"

I didn't want any more to drink. But it was very difficult to say no. I nodded in a half-committal fashion and continued talking.

"I am shocked every day that they allow and pay me to do the work that I do. From the time that I went into my first mind, I was addicted."

"What about it is so addicting?" Commander Bryant asked me. I could look in his eyes and see the honest bewilderment upon his face. It felt good to know, that I could be something more than this man who seemed to be born into royalty.

"It's hard to explain really. First there's the drugs. The cocktail that is approved by the Tribunal brings about a euphoria that just about melts away any and all stress from the inner reality of the indulger. The therapist and patient do not take the same drugs, let me tell you. Most of the time, the patient is taking something that will relax them and combat against anxiety that more than likely will arise during the session."

"And sessions consist of long walks through the mind of the patient?"

"Essentially, yes. I act as Virgil to the disturbed Dante's of this land. Hand in hand, together we roam the dark foliage separating the ocean from the great pyramid holding the individual's life force. The very essence of a person's existence. You see this life force," I was starting to get into the explanation of thought therapy. "We all have one. It's the pulse that threads together the universe."

"Yes, it's this life force that is at the heart of the matter when it comes to the Tribunal?"

"How so?"

"The Tribunal collects lifeforce to soothe the cravings of the Fire Demon they serve."

"Wait, what?"

"They drain the life out of people and feed what comes out to the Fire Demon, who they signed themselves over to. Where do you think the Rim comes from? How do you think they are able to do what they are able to do? They receive power from a Fire Demon and in return have to feed it copious amounts of lifeforce in order to keep it satisfied. Hence the implants, to a certain extent," Commander Bryant said tapping the back of his ear.

Suddenly, it all became clear to me. We were allowed to do whatever we wanted because our lifeforce was being drained by the Tribunal, courtesy of the implants sewn into our brains. No wonder why no one else in the world wanted an implant.

Commander Bryant continued. "Anyway, as you were saying, you help people by going into their minds with them and guide them to their enlightenment."

Very nicely put, Commander.

"Is this therapy really that effective?"

"That's a great question. No, it's not. It's really dangerous in fact. I've had two patients in the last ten years overdose."

"That's awful," the Commander said showing for the first time yet another emotion on his face besides that condescending smirk.

"Yes, those were very trying periods in my practice. It is so common though that it's actually a good record."

"And yet people still swear by thought therapy?"

"Of course they do. Once you go into your mind, literally into your mind, you never really are quite the same. Reality," I said rubbing my fingers together. "Just never really is quite the same as being inside one's own brain."

"I'm sure the drugs you use don't have an effect?"

"Are you kidding me? The drugs we use are highly addictive, and damn good too. It's really about how bad do you want to see your own enlightenment."

"But you can't take it with you when you return from inside of your mind," Commander Bryant said.

"Exactly right, Commander. And that is why they keep coming back. Once you see what is inside of you, you're going to be thirsty for more. And with the drugs, it's an unquenchable desire to grasp an unattainable goal."

"Enlightenment?"

"Well, enlightenment is attainable, just not through thought therapy. The purpose of thought therapy has always been to provide a glimpse at the potential for infinite greatness that lays dormant within every individual. So that they can presumably go after it in their real lives."

"Better themselves?" Commander Bryant asked.

"Yea and get the confidence to believe they can actually do it."

"Just, the drugs defeat the purpose," Commander Bryant said, that beautiful smile appearing on his face again.

"Yea, something like that."

"And you, how do you deal with the drugs you have to take?"

"With great difficulty and focus I'm afraid, Commander," I said and watched as the memories raced through all of the dark and lonely nights wandering through the dark dank forest in my mind. Lost as I was it was best never to let on to the truth. We are always lost. Just lying in the middle of the ocean bobbing up and down on a surf board, waiting for the right wave to push you in."

"Shall we go to the roof?" Commander Bryant interjected, perhaps seeing me drift away into my thoughts. "I keep a greenhouse up there. Since we have time."

Scrunching up my face in pleasant surprise I nodded in agreement that I would like to see the Commander's greenhouse on the roof. Walking up a white narrow spiral staircase we emerged into a large glass green house that seemed to span the entire width of the large building. The view was magnificent. Where the stairs open up at was at the very top of the greenhouse. I put my hands on the ceiling and looked at the orange clouds being painted by the sun setting behind them.

Below us, it looked like a jungle had been growing at the top of the CSD headquarters as every assortment imaginable of plants, flowers, and I was not sure what else, was spread almost as far as I could see. It was as if an entire floor in the building were gutted and only one giant room were made. That is what the greenhouse seemed to be.

I followed the Commander down another narrow white spiral staircase that emptied us out into what was clearly labeled the Herbs section. The woodchips paved paths and mazes through the guided tour of the greenhouse. Showing off all the different species growing, the Commander had designed the greenhouse into his own personal museum. As the sun set my mind raced on and on about Vladimir Fortune, the man that could remember his past lives.

As we perused the Commander's greenhouse, he began to share with me about growing up as a child of the greatest admiral the Company Security Division ever had.

"Admiral Granite was a hard man," the Commander started without prompt after several moments had passed. "He never allowed me to call him dad. I was to address him the same way as every single person that ever spoke to him did. Admiral Granite demanded perfection. This harsh upbringing never seemed like anything other than the greatest nurturing, to me. I remember the very first time he took me beyond the rim to hunt a Bear-Wolf that had been created during the countries' fascination with fusion mutations. I don't know if you've ever seen a Bear-Wolf but they are very large, very fast and have very sharp claws and teeth. Excellent killing machines."

"How old were you when Admiral Granite took you beyond the rim to go Bear-Wolf hunting?" I asked.

"I think I was somewhere around 9 or 10 years of age," Commander Bryant said stretching his lips and smiling. "I had never seen a Bear-Wolf but I had heard a lot about them in school. The kids in my class loved to tell stories about the rumors their fathers tell them while at the dinner table. Admiral Granite knew just where to go to find a Bear-Wolf. He told me he had been tracking this particular Bear-Wolf just for me. The plan was simple. We were to kidnap the Bear-Wolf's cub and use it as bait to lure our hunt into an ambush."

"That seems pretty suicidal against a Bear-Wolf," I said too intrigued to take my eyes off the Commander. We had stopped in front of a group of basil that was exploding from the little cubby holes in the large wooden shelf they were held in. I looked at the basil and wondered what kind of man this Commander Bryant really was. I was about to find out.

"It was suicidal," he answered and continued telling me his story of killing a Bear-Wolf when he was 9 years old. "Or, it would have been suicidal if Admiral Granite wasn't so damn confident in his training of me. The plan worked flawlessly, well almost. The Bear-Wolf got the jump on us and pounced from a thick bush we hadn't taken any attention towards. Admiral Granite saw it first and retreated backwards, leaving me to slay the Bear-Wolf alone. I watched in slow motion as it rose onto its hind legs and leaped at me. The top of its body was large and round with the brown fur of a grizzly. But its face angled out in the shape of a dogs, and its underbelly was slim and muscular. A long tail stretched out behind it darting out like an arrow. As I watched its jaws widen, preparing to sink razor sharp fangs as big as my hand into my neck," Commander Bryant said lifting his large mechanical hand and shaking it. "I thought to myself that this big ugly thing isn't going to think low. I waited until I could feel its hot breath on my face and then sprawled onto my stomach. The Bear-Wolf flew over my head and impaled itself onto the spike we had set up to use when we snuck up on it trying to rescue the cub."

"That sounds pretty lucky," I said disbelieving the simplicity of the ending of what I imagined was going to be an epic story. Possibly the mechanical arm was what I was beginning to become more and more fascinated with. As we walked through the green house, I watched Commander Bryant reaching out and feeling certain plants with it. I was pretty sure that he couldn't feel through the mechanical hand, but I could clearly see that he had some sort of connection with the vegetation on top of the CSD headquarters roof.

"It was incredibly lucky, that's half of what good strategy is. The other half is just being prepared. After I caught my breath and began to understand that I was in the real world, as the adrenalin wore off. Admiral Granite put his hand on my shoulder and pulled me into his massive chest. Besides some foggy memories of him holding me when I was a baby, I couldn't recall Admiral Granite hugging me. I suppose he was happy I hadn't been killed. I'm sure he would have let me die if I wasn't able to defeat the Bear-Wolf."

"But he didn't want you to die."

That smile shined off of Commander Bryant's face. "No, he didn't, and that's why he vigorously trained me so," he said. Commander Bryant then made the face we all in the UCA know well when someone is receiving a phone call. Raising the mechanical arm, I wanted to know how he had gotten, he tapped the implant in the back of his ear.

"Roger that," Commander Bryant said after a dramatic silence ensued over a couple of seconds. "Lockdown's over," he said and looked at me with a smile. Why don't we go get something to eat and we can talk some more about your thought therapy sessions with Vladimir."

I hadn't particularly wanted to do much more for the rest of the day but take a shower and lie in bed. Commander Bryant had cleared my regular scheduled patients using a CSD executive order. Not seeing patients meant I hadn't taken the drugs I usually did for the day. No matter how strong of a thought therapist one could be, it was impossible to fight against chemistry. I needed a fix, and I wasn't sure how much longer I was going to be able to go without one.

Commander Bryant using his observational skills, I'm sure he acquired while getting his arm ripped off and replaced with a mechanical prosthetic, took notice and rightly assumed I was in need of some medicine.

"What do you take?" He asked me straight-faced and direct.

"Sprinkles," I replied, seeing no reason to lie, as he was so interested.

"I figured as much. As I'm sure you know, drug addiction among thought therapist is a rather well-known phenomenon. Especially with us working in government, we take a special interest in thought therapists."

"Yes, I am very well aware of the Tribunal's arrangement with our practice," I said, not hiding my disgust. I didn't care whether he was going to give me a hit or not.

"I hope you know your cooperation is greatly appreciated. I do believe we have come to that point where we must solidify our partnership before we will be able to go forward," and on cue that damn smile sparkled again.

"What do you mean?" I sheepishly asked.

"What I mean is, that in order for me to give you this," Commander Bryant said removing a small plastic bag filled to the brim with sprinkles from his uniformed pants pocket. "I will need to read you in on classified material and therefore will have to deputize you to the ranking of honorary Commander."

"Honorary?" I asked foolishly beginning to feel slighted.

"Well, you haven't seen any combat," he said holding up his mechanical hand and admiring the motions of the different pieces reacting to his twinkling fingers.

He had a point. "How do we do that then?" I asked beginning to accept that there was no way out of this and counting my blessings that I was on the positive end of the receiving stick in my coerced cooperation.

"With some of your blood of course," Commander Bryant answered without blinking.

"My blood?" I asked shocked.

"Yes, the Tribunal demands it. Blood is the only way to sign a partnership into reality."

"And this ties me to the Fire Demon I imagine," I said with a hint of sarcasm on my tongue.

"Doctor Cane, I would think you understood by now that we are all tied to the Fire Demon. You just happen to be in the rare populace possessing knowledge of the Fire Demon."

"I still don't know much about it."

"Knowing of its existence is more than most of the entire world knows. You should count yourself as privileged. And now you're about to enter into a realm of reality you hadn't known existed so close to your own."

"But I have to sign in blood?"

"Yes," Commander Bryant said, removing a small black, hand pouch. When he unzipped and opened the pouch a metal cylinder no larger than a pen rested on a black cushion, along with a thin tube with a needle sticking out of the end. He removed them both and held up the needle end of the plastic tube in his mechanical hand. "This goes into your arm. And then we take your blood."

"And then you hand over the bag of sprinkles?" I asked, looking at the pocket he had put them back into when he pulled out the black pouch.

"We fill this up," he said waving the pen sized metal cylinder, "and then it's all yours."

I considered this without putting myself through the torment of looking at the Commander's grin, but I knew it was there. I went into myself and did a damage assessment. Withdrawal in its beginning stages can cause a great deal of organ damage, irreparable sometimes. I let the greenhouse we were standing in fade away as I went deeper into my mind. Blackness overtook my vision, and quiet returned to me. When I opened my eyes inside of myself, I saw Sifu Ping standing before me. He was dressed in his usual bright red robe that he wore to protect him from something he called the Yipp. I had never the occasion to see it, but I knew Sifu Ping was afraid of it and that was enough for me.

His face was covered by a matching red scarf and only his green eyes stared at me.

"This is an important decision you are faced with," Sifu Ping said to me. "I'm not sure if you are ready."

"That's not very encouraging, Sifu," I said.

"I am not here to encourage you," Sifu Ping sternly replied. "I am here to warn you. Once you go down this path, you will not be able to return from it. Forward is the only way you will be able to go."

"Isn't that always the case, Sifu?"

"Yes, it is. However, this path holds with it a loss I do not think you are willing to take."

"Doesn't seem like I have much of a choice," I said.

"You're always so foolish for being so bright," Sifu Ping said to me.

He was usually right. But this time, I really couldn't see a way out. I wish now sitting in this cell, writing this letter to you, I had taken a few more moments and found that other path that I couldn't see right away at first. Sprinkles is a hell of a drug though, and I didn't care about the warning coming from my mind disguised as Sifu Ping.

"So, what's it going to be?" Commander Bryant said pulling me out of myself and back to reality. I found that we had returned to the office and were standing by the fireplace. A new glass of whiskey was in my hand. I felt the warmth of the fire roasting against my right pants leg. I took a long sip of whiskey and felt the liquid warm its way down my throat and into my belly, soothingly expanding it.

"Just don't take too much," I said rolling up my sleeve and revealing the nook on the other side of my elbow. Commander Bryant stuck the needle in with no type of finesse and the pen sized metallic cylinder began to omit a sucking noise. It wasn't long before I was watching my blood snake its way out of my arm and through the plastic tubing. I had taken a seat in the chair Commander Bryant had been sitting in earlier, when I was telling him of myself and thought therapy. Once the cylinder was filled, the Commander removed the tubbing and returned it to the black hand pouch. He then put my blood into the jacket pocket of his uniform, for safe keeping I imagine.

"Here you go, a deal's a deal," Commander Bryant said tossing me the bag of sprinkles that had been in the pants pocket I had been trying to not beam a hole into with my eyes.

Catching the bag with reflexes faster than I imagined the Bear-Wolf had—maybe it wouldn't have been impaled if it did have them—I tore it open and poured out the sprinkles onto the coffee table sitting before me. Removing the metal file I kept on me at all times, I kept a lot of patients most days, I started to break up the pile of sprinkles into five lines as thick as fingers. I slowly inhaled the first line, savoring the journey from start to finish. My mind instantly snapped back to when my father got his foot caught in the mouse trap when I was in grammar school.

Transported back to $3^{rd}$ or $4^{th}$ grade, the winter had swept through our region of the country and the roaches, mice, and rats had nowhere to escape for shelter. Our warm family home became a perfect place for the nearby mice. The presence of rodents in the house drove my father up the wall and through the roof with anger. To think that they would be this direct and disrespectful as to squat in his home would be his thought. My father took his ownership of property seriously at all times.

He invested in some ancient looking traps that you see in a Tom and Jerry cartoon. Sprinkling a trail of rice around it, my dad tucked it into a corner in the kitchen just before we all went to bed. Very strictly he warned my brother and me to be careful if we decided to get up in the middle of the night for a snack or to pee. Clapping his hands together loudly he said that if one of our toes got caught in the clasp of the trap, we would have to be rushed to the emergency room to hopefully save whatever toe had been caught. Suffice it to say, when we went to sleep me nor my brother had any intention to rise up before the sun peeked its head over the horizon to start the day.

The sudden roar of our father's yell broke our nighttime reverie. Rushing into the kitchen we were met with a scene that mixed together both comedy and tragic drama in a grand unfolding fashion. Our father had been very correct, and he was not lucky enough to keep his toe.

As I relived the event, my eyes rolled back into place and I began to breathe again.

"Feel better?" Commander Bryant said sitting in the seat opposite the other side of the coffee table.

"Yes, much better. Are you going to join me?" I asked taking notice of Deputy Shadow that must have returned while I was flying into my first pick-me-up of the day; and late in the day it was to be just starting out. Up until that point I had attended to my schedule with great efficiency and I took great pride in the fact that I was a professional, and trained very well to be one. I still take pride in it, even now as I sit in this cage awaiting my execution.

Commander Bryant raised his mechanical hand in refusal and said no thank you. I was more than fine with that. From the looks of it, I thought to myself, I was going to be spending the rest of the night and maybe well into the next morning with, Commander Bryant, stuck with the switchblade grin.

I shook my head clear of all excess thoughts and got down to the business of snorting this second line. By the end of the 4th I was just where I wanted to be and ready to take on whatever the hell the Commander had in store for me. Little did I know that Father Clementine would later reveal to me just how little I knew about what was going on and why the memories and thought therapy sessions of Vladimir Fortune contained the clue to defeat the Fire Demon.

Commander Bryant and I had been talking for I don't know how long, being on sprinkles alters time significantly. Before I realized that, however, my thought therapy hat was beginning to kick in. The Commander had been talking some more about this childhood and the altered course in his life following his father, Admiral Granite's death.

"The fact that he died really confused me. It shouldn't have but it did. For some reason, the idea that he could die just didn't make sense to me."

I nodded my head in understanding and said, "That makes a great deal of sense. Often times when one views a parental figure as invincible, to see them die is devastating and the brain has trouble compensating with the change in reality as it had been following up until that point."

"That's psychobabble," the Commander spat dismissing my attempted words of comfort. "I didn't look at Admiral Granite as invincible. He was a flesh and blood man; I knew this without a doubt. It was this fact that made him even more of an impenetrable human being. The number of flaws that he contained within his heart were astronomically vast and it's a testament to the discipline and will he radiated almost supernaturally. That is why I was so shook when he died of a heart attack. To die of such a petty thing, as well," Commander Bryant said, disgust clearly smacked across his face.

"Admiral Granite never got to see me graduate from the academy either," the Commander continued. "I knew he was looking forward to it with his entire being. Somehow, I feel like him dying of a heart attack was my fault in some way."

"I don't understand how you can say such a thing," I responded to the Commander. I was genuinely shocked at his statement.

"I was held back a year," he said quickly explaining. "I had a six-month period where I started to rebel for no reason. I drank and did drugs and very quickly was put on probation. I violated that and right before I was to be expelled, Admiral Granite intervened and pulled me out on 'official business.' Then he threw me on a boat with a crew of the CSD's top Special Forces officers that were conducting surveillance in the South China Sea's. I became their bitch and learned very quickly the value of education and the privilege I had been handed as my birthright. I got my act together and there was never any discussion about it between us, the Admiral and me. But I was a year behind. And in some ways, sometimes, I blame myself for making his heart bad."

I said nothing. The Commander sat with his head looking down into his hands that had been resting in his lap for quite some time. I watched as he drifted from the large office we had spent the better half of the day in, far away into what I imagined were his memories. The pull to engage him in thought therapy rose to a nag and eventually became a nervous pang in my belly, pulsing along with my rapid heartbeat.

"Have you ever done thought therapy, Commander?" I asked on a whim after several moments had passed. (Well, whatever, I was on sprinkles).

He continued looking at his hands as they rested in his lap. I knew that he had heard me though. A look flashed across the Commanders face that I had seen many times before on first time patients.

A beautiful crack of thunder suddenly elated the sky outside of the CSD headquarters. For the first time I saw Commander Bryant caught off guard. He seemed to regress back into that little boy that had walked beyond the rim with his father. The moment didn't last long and the Commander returned was to his same stoic features. The smile I had come to admire was nowhere to be seen on his face, however.

Schubert's Fantasy in F minor had been playing through the overhead speakers, for once again I have no idea how long. Damn sprinkles make keeping track of time so difficult. Being inside of a patient's mind, it's an entirely different thing, however. Time evaporates into an unknown entity and the wondrous globe we exist in fades away when you enter a brain.

There is no sound for time. Then, without warning, a great cacophony of noise issues forth from every direction. Blinding the senses and with ears bleeding, the virtual reality construct comes into birth. It's always amusing to watch as patients observe time bleeding away, and begin to realize that they are inside of their own minds. It's not a pleasant thing often times enough, I explained to Commander Bryant as he continued to study his hands resting in his lap.

"It's at this point," I continued. "That the needs of the physical world fade away for the patient and they lean back into the trust of their thought therapist."

With this the Commander raised his head and looked into my eyes. They glistened in the florescent lights that were hanging besides the Boss speakers bringing Schubert's Fantasy in F minor to an end. Silence brought its eerie presence into the scene and wafted a glimpse of the melancholy I've come to know quite intimately at the time of this writing, across the moving picture taking place before me.

"And then what happens?" Commander Bryant asked me.

"And then, we begin the therapy. Most minds require some sort of pathway that must be traversed or a large series of steps that must be either walked up or down."

"Steps like a test?" Commander Bryant asked.

"No," I responded. "Literally steps that the patient and the guide must walk down or up in order for the journey to even begin. Seems our minds inherently know to make the beginning difficult."

"Weed out the weak," Commander Bryant said with the famous smile slowly making its return appearance.

"Something like that," I responded.

The soundtrack filling the office I had spent the better part of my entire day in shifted pace. A rendition of Ave Maria I had never heard before started to play from the speakers above. The tragedy of the little boy's voice echoed volumes throughout the Commanders office. I should have taken notice that the Commander's shadow that had been with us every moment since I met Admiral Granite's son, had been with us every step—an entire revolution of the way throughout the trip down memory lane about Vladimir Fortune. He had left the office.

In actuality it wasn't much of a surprise that Deputy Shadow had faded into obscurity as I had just one of the five thick lines of sprinkles. I had signed in blood to obtain what's left on the coffee table before me. Feeling just about ready, I snorted up the last of the sprinkles.

The inside of my nose pulsed and I felt as each grain of the substance made its way up my nostrils and into my blood stream. I closed my eyes and allowed the time to pass over us both, however long it turned out to be. When I opened my eyes, the Commander was staring at me.

I looked back at him knowing not what to say. My mind was racing as the high of the sprinkles attached itself onto me. Then I saw that familiar glint of puzzlement inside the orb of Commander Bryant's pupils and knew what he wanted.

"Would you like to try thought therapy?" I casually asked.

"Yes, I would," Commander Bryant answered with very little hesitation.

And thus, our sessions began.

"Ok then, we're going to have to go to my office. And I'm going to need some more sprinkles," I said spreading my hands before the coffee table with single grains of sprinkles scattered about.

"I can do you one better," Commander Bryant said just as Deputy Shadow reappeared with a metal suitcase in his hand. Placing the suitcase gently on the coffee table before me, the Deputy slid the two clasps on either side of the handle open and lifted the lid of the suitcase. A perfect thought therapy starter kit was revealed to be inside.

Off and on the strong patter tap of rain drops hitting hard above could be heard as Deputy Shadow made his exit. *Miles Davis' Kind of Blue* softly blared waves of sound from the overhead speakers as I thought about what to do. It wasn't that I did not know what to do. Things were just happening so fast.

Sifu Ping's voice could be heard echoing in my mind. "Get to work, stupid," it said.

"Let's get you set up," I said clapping my hands together and rubbing them as if to produce a spark of fire from wet tinder.

When the Commander had all the proper electrodes attached to his chest and temple, I injected him with 10ml of Sleepy milk. If it were anything like the quality of the bag of sprinkles I had earlier, I was sure the Commander was in for a wild ride. I placed the virtual reality headset over him and watched as Commander Bryant relaxed into the leather chair he was seated in. The electrodes and headset were connected wirelessly to the mainframe built into the suitcase. I clicked the power button on and waited for the involuntary jerk to signal that the patient was standing by in the loading room.

The commander jerked and then calmed down. I took two lines and plugged in.

◆

As always, darkness met me as the program began to load up. The screen of my vision illuminated and white light fields were all I could see. Once I felt the ground beneath my feet, I knew that I was in the loading room. A bewildered Commander Bryant I found staring down the endless staircase that lead into his mind. I tapped him on the back and startled an uncharacteristic jump from him. The Commander turned to me and smiled.

"Are you ready for this?" I asked putting my hand on his nearest shoulder. Silently nodding, I put one foot in the front of the other and set out down the stairs into Commander Bryant's mind.

Glancing at my Hamilton wristwatch, I took note that it was approximately 1:03 in the morning. We had an hour before the drugs began to wear off. I knew from experience that it's best to be back in the loading room when that occurred. The mind was not a nice place to be in when coming down off drugs.

I could hear Commander Bryant's steady footsteps echoing on the stone steps as we climbed down them. Behind me was a man that knew just how to tame fear and I was impressed with how he maintained his composure. Most patients aren't able to walk down the steps of their own accord because of fear. I've had a few patients that weren't even able to get out of the loading room. Those were wasted sessions that I usually spent seated in the lotus contemplation. This session, however, I knew was going to be once in a lifetime special. Increasing my pace, I began leaping skipping four or five stairs at a time to start the journey as the guide to Commander Bryant's enlightenment.

We reached the last stair around 1:15am. The giant wooden green door stood before us.

There is always a door after the last step. No one door is ever the same, however. And it is only through this door that an individual can enter their minds. Only the patient can open the door, and only a guide knows what to do from then on. A series of tasks must be performed in sequence or else the mind will close up and we will be booted out and be forced to climb the steps to the loading room and await the exit jerk that pulls patients out of the drug induced coma they fall in.

The Commander's door was very old but had been kept in pristine condition. The shape of the door was oval, not rectangular, and stood taller than both of us, if one stood on the other's shoulders and stretched their fingers high overhead. We stood before the massive structure in silence and I watched as Commander Bryant went about processing how best to get into whatever was behind the giant green door, ultimately being his mind.

"So, what do we do?" Commander Bryant finally asked after several minutes had passed of him feeling, knocking, smelling and tasting the green wooden door that acted as the entrance into his mind.

"You open the door," I responded.

Commander Bryant looked at me as every patient I have had has done over the last 10 years. Yes, I nodded and pointed my chin in the direction of the brass doorknob besides his arm.

"It's just that easy?" he asked me with skepticism on his face, that grin not far behind.

"Just that easy," I said floating on autopilot. Stretching my neck from side-to-side, I limbered up for the run that was approaching. Commander Bryant didn't know but he took notice of my preparation and that smile flashed across his face.

"Very well then," he said and grabbed ahold of the doorknob twisted and opened the passageway into his brain.

The Chet Baker Quartet album, 'No problem,' vibrated into our ears becoming the soundtrack to the therapy session. Everyone has a soundtrack. Some have multiple soundtracks behind multiple doors. Commander Bryant wasn't as insecure as all that. One door and one soundtrack were all that was needed. Though, I learned not to count on any consistencies to occur while acting as guide to individuals walking through their own minds.

As the door pushed open to a full stop, I waited for the Commander to take the first lean in. A dozen steps later, we were standing in a land of magic.

Commander Bryant was a romantic to the core. Elegance and simplicity floated over and painted the muscled skeleton of his identity. We found ourselves on an empty beach with a forest of tall trees tucked away just beyond the horizon line. The soft cool breeze bounced off of the ocean at our backs and hit my face just as the ebb and flow of the waves registered in my ears. We stood barefoot, both in beige shorts and loose-fitting button up tees. The sand beneath our feet was a highlighter pink. Stretching as far as the eye could see, I squished the grains between my toes and felt the warmth of the sun heating each one.

Turning to face the ocean, I was met with a bright green, where blue waves should've been. I pulled a piece of red vine liquorish from my pocket and began to gnaw at it as I contemplated the sea. I always carried red vines when inside of a mind during a thought therapy session. For no reason other than I enjoyed red vines and they were good to eat while thinking.

When I was younger you couldn't keep me away from candy. I was an addict to say the least. Old habits die hard, I guess. I felt Commander Bryant began to stir beside me. It was time to begin our journey into his mind.

"Are you ready, Commander?" I asked him.

He nodded his head and said yes.

The growl I heard but didn't comprehend. Commander Bryant's highly attuned sense trained to a razor-sharp degree, detected and assessed the danger apparent and changed his face to a hardened statue of determination. Pushing me to the highlighter pink sand, I caught a glimpse of the smile I came to love and hate flashed across his face. He sprang with lightning speed towards where the growl originated. As I followed his large frame soar through the air, the threat became apparent. A large Bear-Wolf had got the drop on us while I was lagging, admiring the shores of Commander Bryant's mind.

As the two clashed into one giant force of violence, the Bear-Wolf struck Commander Bryant in the face. Toppling him over on his back, a follow through roll was all it took for the Commander to be back on his feet and on the defensive. The Bear-Wolf wasted no time and launched a series of vicious snaps from his long fangs, as its massive frame nimbly danced through the sand.

Commander Bryant dodged and defected these with ease. I rose my pathetic self from the highlighter pink sand and brushed my hands clean, watching the scene before me knowing there was more danger ahead.

While I briefly contemplated the future, the Commander was engaged in the moment. The Bear-Wolf doubled back and began to stalk its prey. The initial attack had proved two worthy adversaries were engaged. A silent bubble of respect appeared from the exchange of energy between the two. Bursting abruptly as unknown numbers of moments passed, a light expanded and then engulfed the three of us. A vacuum of decision was created as the moment of life falling into death waved hello.

In a flash I watched as the Bear-Wolf stared into the Commanders eyes, hovering close to its own. It hadn't even registered it was dead when it collapsed to the sand.

I wasn't even sure where he got the blade from. Drips of blood from the knife Commander Bryant pulled from somewhere, and used to stab the Bear-Wolf in the neck, splattered onto the sand, mixing into the highlighter pink. He wiped it clean on his beige shorts covered thigh and replaced it into his back pocket. Commander Bryant looked at me and nodded to see if I was ok. I responded that I was with a similar nod.

"We should carve it up and bury what we don't need. If there's one Bear-Wolf, there will be another. Judging from the size of this one, its absence will be noticed," Commander Bryant said grabbing the Bear-Wolf by the hind legs and dragging it toward the forest that was some distance away from the green waves lightly crashing behind us.

I followed behind the trail of blood and sand the head and body the Bear-Wolf made, as the Commander dragged it onward. We came to the base of where the forest began, which was much larger and deeper than what had initially appeared after we walked through the Commander's large wooden green door marking the entrance into his mind.

I watched him start a fire, carve up the Bear-Wolf, dig a large hole and methodically go through what I imagine his father Admiral Granite had drilled into him to do. I basked in the excellence being exhibited before me. By the time he was finished, the sun had begun to set. Though it was past 1 in the morning when we began the thought therapy, the sun had been high in the sky when we found ourselves on the beach.

I hadn't noticed if music had been playing before or after the exchange with the Bear-Wolf we had unexpectedly partook upon. But I did take notice to the sax of *John Coltrane's Blue Train* coming through from invisible speakers in the cloudless yellow sky. Colors were always a relative thing in every patient's mind I acted as a guide through. The Commander was one of those rare sorts that didn't require much walkthrough. Grasping the bull by the horns, we dove into the forest with no fear, once he had finished collecting all the pieces of his rightfully earned prize Bear-Wolf.

The soft tantalizing sounds of Coltrane whisked away any doubts. There aren't ever any doubts really while I'm engaged in thought therapy that may have been teeter-tottering on forming as we traversed deeper and deeper into the dank foliage. Darkness became the norm after a short time and the sun that had made its retreat some time just before we entered the jungle had fully clocked out by the time we reached the first sign of life.

"I know this place," the Commander said walking up to the small cottage we happened upon. The foliage had begun to disperse and we were following a trail when the smoke from the chimney of the hut, Commander Bryant said he recognized, came into view. "Yea, this is my grandmother's house," he said with a child's smile I hadn't yet seen shinning across his face. "I spent every spring here," he said walking straight up to the front door of the small cottage. "There were a lot of kids whose mothers and fathers were in the CSD," I could sense the sentimentality arising in Commander Bryant's voice. It was never this easy I thought as he knocked on the door.

Coltrane picked up his pace and the flutter of fingers hitting keys on the sax clustered together into glorious music. Commander Bryant stood behind the door, lost in between his childhood and the moment, waiting for his grandmother to open the door. She did not disappoint. There was an ominous creek as the door began to open. A small old woman with hollow eyes, wearing a brown tunic cautiously and suspiciously peered her wrinkled face out from the doorway.

"My grandson," she said unsurprised to see Commander Bryant standing before her. The tiny wrinkled woman grasped the Commander by the face and pulled him down to her level. He complied without fuss and she gave him kisses and shook his face. For no reason it seemed, the soundtrack playing through the invisible speakers in the sky changed back to *Chet Baker*. This time the album *Strollin'* from the year 1986 began to play.

"Come in, come in," the commander's grandmother said. "And bring your friend too," she said motioning towards me and walking away from the open door into her small cottage. The Commander waved his hand towards himself and offered me entry in. I followed him and closed the door behind me.

Once inside, the small cottage was about what I had expected it to be. Complete with the cast iron cauldron bubbling and spurting whatever the hell his grandmother had been cooking before we came in. Being short, the cottage was an ok height for me, with the ceiling of the adobe structure being just out of reach of my extended hand above my head. The Commander wasn't the correct fit for the tight quarters though. This only enhanced the cuteness of the scene unfolding before me, however.

The small wrinkled woman in the brown tunic went about preparing a space in her humble dwelling for the two of us to make ourselves comfortable in. We politely obliged and rested while drinking tea and observing the woman as she continued to go about her routine. It seemed as if she had anticipated our arrival, or had everything on hand for the arrival of unexpected guests. With ease and delicacy, Commander Bryant's grandmother raced about her minuscule kitchen that doubled as the dining room bedroom we sat in, and prepared a magnificent feast.

After munching down on what I could of dessert, the Commanders grandmother looked at us both and her eyes suddenly turned red. She stared and we watched as the unblinking eyes of the wrinkled old woman began to cry tears of blood, forming puddles into her hands catching them.

The Commander started to rise and rush towards his grandmother but I grabbed his arm and pulled on it, returning him down to his seat.

"What're you doing?" he snapped at me.

"Just wait," I said to him having seen something similar to this happen once before.

Chet Baker's horn began to fade away as the bloody tears from Commander Bryant's grandmother did not cease to fall. Silence made its way into the small cottage following the last blare heard of the trumpet. The soft melodic wine echoed in my ear's imagination.

"Everything's fine," I said trying to calm the Commander, who was beginning to be visibly shaken. "Remember, this is your mind. None of this is real. It's of the utmost importance that you do not forget this while we are on our journey to find your enlightenment."

The Commander closed his eyes and nodded in understanding. No matter how many minds I go into, it always takes just a matter of time before the subconscious of the patient begins to test their belief of reality.

The first thing you see is always the earliest memory stored inside of the database sitting within us all. For Commander Bryant, it had been his grandmother. I'm not all that sure what the bleeding eyes were about but I didn't pay much attention to it. The mind had a great flair for the dramatic, I've learned over my decades of guiding patients through their thought therapy sessions. I wish I had paid attention to it.

It took a bit more pulling, but I was able to get the Commander out of the small cottage and we were back on the path, traveling deeper into the dense foliage growing thicker with each step. I glanced at my Hamilton wristwatch and saw that it was 1:25am. We had plenty of time, I thought, as we came upon a large open space where the trees extended to the clouds and the sun peaked through in large cracks between leaves. 21 dead horses scattered the field. Each with the distinct markings of death by disease. A stale rotting stench made its way into our nostrils and we both recoiled, holding back vomit.

Carefully weaving our way through the carcasses, with burning eyes and searing throats, the commander and I made it to the other side where the path began again and the foliage seemed to grow thicker, the area darker. Even deeper into the woods we went.

I had never been much of a fan of forest or jungles. Camping was never my thing. I could see by that stupid smile the Commander seemed to throw on just for me, that he was enjoying himself.

"Did you go camping much as a kid?" I asked the Commander as boredom began to set in. Even though the Hamilton wristwatch I wore continued to register time in the same normal way as outside the

Commander's mind, there was no real way of telling how long it had been since we began. Nor was there any way to know how long it would take to reach his enlightenment.

"I wouldn't quite call it camping," the Commander responded chuckling to himself. "More like boot camps. I went to a lot of boot camps growing up."

"Jeez, what was that like?" I asked grimacing at how awful that sounded.

"Wasn't that bad. I was something of a celebrity because of the Admiral. This did well in the commons with the other cadets. But it didn't do well for me when it came to our instructors. They were determined to break Admiral Granite's son."

"To toughen you up? Make sure you didn't go spoiled on them?" I asked.

"Hell no. Most people hated the Admiral. He was too perfect, raised the bar too high. Most of his career was spent defending dirty attacks on his character and sabotage was so common, the Admiral became a master at deflecting it. No, they gave me shit because they wanted to embarrass the Admiral. Funny thing is, even if they had succeeded in breaking me, the Admiral wouldn't have cared one bit. He would've said that was the flaw of my mother's side. Only greatness ran in his blood," Commander Bryant said with a faraway look on his face.

"Charming," I responded.

"Yes, very. That was the Admiral. Just a bundle of joy 24 hours a day 7 days a week," the Commander sarcastically said. "The survival tests were always my favorite thing to do. Because the instructors didn't give a fuck about me, and after a while I grew tired of their torment. So, I vanished into the survival section of the camp and never reappeared until the Admiral came to collect me at the end of the semester. It became a thing after I did it the first year. The Admiral got such a kick out of when he pulled up in the CSD limousine and the instructors stuttered out that they had lost his son."

"How did he react?" I asked holding up a large tree trunk that had fallen and blocked the pathway, for the Commander to walk under. He returned the favor and the heavy dead wood returned to the dirt path with a loud thud that reverberated a bit louder than I had thought it would.

"He knew I wasn't lost. I always kept direct correspondence with the Admiral. He insisted upon reports three times a day. I got used to it. All of these little things he did forged me into the man I am today."

"Then, why aren't you an Admiral yet?" I asked the question suddenly popping into my head.

That damn smile appeared on his face again. He didn't say anything at first, just smiled as we walked along the thick foliage covered path. The sun had not made an appearance for quite a while. As I said, time inside of the mind was not something that could be counted on to be consistent with reality. Time here was different.

# Chapter Five:
## Rah Pooh

Rah Pooh. The name meant nothing to me, but it meant a lot to the Commander. As we trekked farther into the dense vegetation of Commander Bryant's mind, we could hear the name whispered along each leaf that wisped past us.

Rah Pooh.

Rah Pooh.

For the longest I thought I was hearing rat poo. But as I rightly assumed, that was incorrect. The name came and went along the wind, whispering soft nothings, promising everything.

After the voice chanting its own name came to be beyond what could be dealt with, I asked Commander Bryant if he knew what it meant. That wonderful smile flashed across his face again.

"Yes, I know what that is," he responded slightly nodding his head as he did so.

"What is it?" I asked brushing aside some foliage that was blocking the way. We came upon a large stone structure with a single doorway to walk through. From the outside it looked like a giant stone cube. It was very old. The Soulful Piano of Junior Mance began to play from the invisible speakers above. The Commander and I both stared at the structure listening.

"I guess we've got to go in there," Commander Bryant said, beginning to move forward.

I glanced at my Hamilton wristwatch. It was 1:45am, about time for the thought therapy session to be wrapping up. The cold chill of urgency started to crawl up my spine as we walked through the doorway and succumbed upon the massive weight of the space. The opening we walked through that had no door suddenly sealed us in with a massive vacuum suck seal emphasizing that there was no exit from this structure.

Commander Bryant glanced at me with a hint of nervousness splashed across his face. I did my best imitation of his slick smile and said, "Nothing to fear, in 15 minutes back in the real world, the systems exit procedure will click on, and our drugs will begin to wear off. Before we know it, we'll find ourselves back in the loading room."

I'm not sure if this brought any calm to Commander Bryant but he nodded his head like a good solider and carried on confidently forward. In the very center of the massively open and empty structure, with ceilings that seemed to stretch higher than could be seen, a sphere the size of a bowling ball floated and glowed, surrounded by a sparkly haze of energy omitting from the object.

"Is that?" Commander Bryant stuttered out as he asked

"Yes, it's your enlightenment," I responded thinking on the countless times I have said this very same remark.

"What do I do now?" the commander asked, unconsciously shuttling his feet forward inching closer to the gold sphere with lightening bolting from it.

"Now, you grab ahold of your enlightenment for as long as you can and absorb from it what you can," I'd said this quite a few times as well.

The Commander looked at me with bewildered eyes, and amazingly sweat had begun to perspire from his brow. I looked at him and could see that young boy that had killed his first Bear-Wolf shine his innocent eyes through the hardened shell of what was now Commander Bryant.

"It's ok, Commander," I said smiling and nodding my head. "You can do this. This is just a single step. Nothing to fear."

The mention of fear seemed to snap him back to his battle-scarred self. Nodding his head in thanks, the Commander increased his pace and his gait forward became more confident. As he reached out his hands to grab the yellow sphere of lightening that was his enlightenment, I glanced at my wristwatch. 1:55am, just enough time for him to get a taste, I thought, as his hands gripped the object.

Lightening sparked and bolts shot out from all sides. I watched a great many, after having gone through whatever path their mind devised to get to this point, drop their enlightenment for fear of being electrocuted. When that happens, the connection is instantly broken and we are transported directly to the loading room. The Commander was no bitch, however.

Lightening encircled him and rhythmically sent surges of electricity throughout him. The Commanders body began to seize and the light sparking off him become so great that I had to shield my eyes from its illumination. As I peeked from between the openings of my finger as my hands covered my eyes, I saw as Commander Bryant's form lifted from the ground we stood upon and began to soar upwards toward the infinite ceiling.

I felt the cold, which had successfully arrived. I watched as my arms began to freeze over and turn into ice. My feet had already been covered, and it didn't take long before I sensed the flow creep of frozen water climb within my stomach and chest. My head freezing was always the part I hated the most about the exit.

◆

When I opened my eyes, Commander Bryant and I were back in the loading room. He was standing staring at his hands, still apart, matching the distance of the sphere he had been holding. A glazed that looked very familiar to me was upon his face. It was the look of drugs wearing off and he was beginning to wake from his coma. I blinked my eyes and when I opened them, I was out of the Commander's mind and back in the office at the top of the CSD headquarters.

I quickly rose from the chair, pulling clear of all the electrodes and virtual reality headset attached, making my way towards Commander Bryant. He jerked once, than twice and began to stir out of the drug induced coma he had voluntarily allowed himself to be placed in. I unhooked him from the electrodes stuck to his head and chest and slowly helped the Commander up into a sitting position. It didn't take him very long to be able to stay on his feet of his own free will.

"How do you feel?" I asked the Commander after he drank a glass of whiskey I poured for him. Adding another for myself, I sipped and patiently waited for him to get his mouth working again.

"I feel alright," he said after gulping down the shot I had poured him. I refilled his and drained mine then refilled my glass as well. Putting the decanter back in its place, I returned to sipping and contemplating. Another mind, another day. This was a saying I took to using once I started my practice of thought therapy. After the initial novelty of gliding through another's mind wears away all that's left to break up the monotony of it are catchy sayings.

I delayed in the after-session protocol and allowed myself a moment to intake the oxygen around me. An overabundance of sage was wafting in the air that I did not take a liking to. Noticing my face contorted in an image of distaste, the Commander walked over towards the large windows and opened a few. The cool breeze of 2 am wafted in. At over 100 stories up, the air mixed with everything it could grasp within the vicinity.

"Are you alright, Doctor Cane?" The Commander asked.

I glanced at him and could barely recognize the distorted face. My vision had begun to fail me. Feeling my body begin to wobble I attempted to regain my balance and could not. Alarm began to overpower me and my face betrayed me, showing the state.

Commander Bryant ran from the window he had opened, catching me just as my legs betrayed me. He lowered me to the white fluffy carpet and I could feel the vibrations of him yelling. I couldn't hear a single word he said. The veins on his neck protruding signaled to me that he was calling for help. This thought comforted me and I began to allow myself to fall into the dream that was pulling so viciously at me.

A violent smack across the face brought sound and feeling back into my reality. Another smack reverberated my cheek as the Commander looked down at me. Eyes fire hot and cool as steel, I glared into the brown orbs feeling anger build within me.

"Doctor Cane, I know you're in there," Commander Bryant was saying. "Stay awake. I think you did too many sprinkles too fast."

I heard this through a muffled distance of recognition. He was right, I thought beginning to feel out my symptoms. I laboriously got my breathing in rhythm and got up off the white fluffy carpet. Embarrassed I mumbled some kind of apology and quickly made my way to the door. At the elevator, I stabbed the call button for the lift repeatedly as Commander Bryant caught up to me. I glanced at him feeling the sweat drip down my backside.

The Commander eyed me with a look of pity I did not appreciate. The elevator doors slid open after a ding of the lift's arrival. I nodded a salute to the Commander and he returned a nod in kind. For a brief second I thought of Rah Pooh and what, or who it was. It mattered not to me. Given the state I was in, all I wanted was to get back down to the street and hop in a trolley towards my condo.

"Tomorrow, we'll need to go through all of your files and records pertaining to Vladimir Fortune," Commander Bryant said to me, squarely eyeing my form, as the elevator doors slid close. Silence engulfed the radius of my hearing into the voice I had tried so hard not to hear from.

"Damn what a party," the voice inside my brain began to say. I felt the lift shake and begin its descent down to the ground level that I had selected on the panel display. Mirrors covered the walls and ceiling with cheap red carpet keeping our shoes warm beneath us. "Where we going to next?" the voice inside me asked.

"Home," I stupidly responded.

"Oh no we are not," the voice said with disgust in its throat. "We are just right and it's not even 2:30am yet, baby. Let's hit them streeeeetttsss." The voice said this with a drawl at the end of 'streets.'

The elevator lift hit the ground floor with a thud and the sliding doors split open. The lobby was eerily empty and instantly the feeling of being very alone overtook me.

"Now I bet you're glad I'm here," the voice said to me as I made my way from the elevator to the main entrance. It made me sad to think that the voice in my head was right.

Pushing the horizontal handle with my hip I glanced over my shoulder at the emptiness of the CSD lobby. Instantly the cool air, after 2 am in the city, hit my face. Acid rain trickled down lightly burning my face. I touched the implant behind me ear and felt the constricted feeling of layers of plastic adhering over every inch of my skin. Glancing at the empty street, I activated my implants GPS with my mind and thought the directions onto the screen that appeared in my vision. A compass appeared floating in front of me, pointing in the correction direction of the walk I had chosen to take.

Walking was the best thing for me after having consuming too much sprinkles. My mental health monitor had been pestering me about taking a vacation and now the memory of our interactions popped up and disappeared in my mind's eye. Bouncing and echoing about through the other noise that was beginning to increase, the voice in my mind got a kick out of all of this.

Its laughter overpowered everything in my head and I stopped walking, waiting for it to finish.

"Would you please stop laughing?" I asked it aloud, raising my voice. At just that moment an old woman walking with a large hump causing her face to hover near her belly button was walking past me. My unnecessary exclamation startled her and I felt ashamed. She scurried off and I appeared in the empty night air as a creepy doctor. No one would've known I was a doctor by the clothes I wore nor the way I walked. This feeling just glared in my mind and made me feel inadequate. It was mostly due to the fact that I had too much sprinkles.

◆

The laughter subsided and the voice in my brain quieted down. Nothing left to say, I thought. I dared not say another word, lest the voice pipe up again. The compass floating before me continued to point in the direction I followed and I observed on a swivel the scene around me. Those living beings that were out on the street had tucked themselves in tightly under their makeshift homes. Shelters consisting of mainly cardboard boxes and newspapers, designed especially to be able to withstand the acid rainstorms, were arranged in a Tetris of ways.

I saw a few heads poke out as my presence passed their front entrances, but not many paid me any attention. The rain continued to lightly pitter-pat upon the plastic coating covering my skin as I walked home. Once reaching my domicile, I touched the implant behind my ear and felt the plastic seep back into my pores and disintegrate into my blood stream. The Tribunal said that the plastic would help to clean our blood of toxins. To their credit, most diseases had been cured. ALS and Parkinson's, for example, were a rarity to be seen.

The automation kicked in a second after registering my implant. Lights turned on at settings suitable to me based on my mood

*John Coltrane's 'Blue Train'* began to play from the Bose speakers wired around the entire condo. The irony of hearing this album again was not lost upon me. At least it's in the real world, I thought to myself as I plopped my form down onto the sofa that had come with the condo. Most of the furniture had come with the purchase I made of the place.

The artificial maid came in with a beer that had been poured into a chilled glass and laid it on the table next to my head where I lay. There wasn't a single drop of foam creeping over the side of the glass. This fascinated me in my exhausted state and I stared at the phenomenon for quite a while.

Sitting up I drained half the cold glass of beer and fell back down to the couch. It wasn't long before I drifted off into a hazy nightmarish dream.

At that point I had only seen the awful image of the Crimson Knight inside of Vladimir Fortune's head. A figure I would come to know intimately as Commander Bryant, and I exchanged all assortments of notes, records and videos we had on Vladimir Fortune. Untold tales unraveled through the complied telling of the story of the man whom remembered his past lives. The Crimson Knight made his appearance that night.

Fire surrounded all that I saw. As the heat baking upon me proved as the reality happening, the armored helmet of the Medieval Knight put its nose upon my own and sharply inhaled. The cold, cold feeling that jolted into my face as I felt the welded metal helmet press into my flesh, seemed to pull the life out of me. I imagined that my face would melt like the Nazi's did at the end of *Indiana Jones and the Raiders of the Lost Ark*. This did not happen.

The Crimson Knight snaked its head left and right in reptile fashion, as it continued to scrutinize me. The flames around and behind it crackled as the stench of the Fire Demon's minion's breath stung the insides of my nostrils. A great shadow engulfed us both and the alarm from the implant behind my ear rang throughout my head. Rising from the sofa I looked around the room and found that I had slept well into the morning. The 10 am, or so, sunlight was shining in through the windows of the middle-floor condo I had held for the last four years.

"You're moving on up," is what my friends and colleagues said to me when I signed the lease. That was when the pain in my kidneys began to lightly flare. The two orbs floating on either side of the lower back of my spine felt as if they were glowing. I was sure my liver didn't look any better, but that mattered not at the moment. I had three messages that I pondered for a moment, as they flashed in the upper display on my right eyeball. All information from the implant came from a Heads-up Display, or HUD that appeared in the right eye.

That is the 3rd dimension of reality as we know it. The inner voice, the fourth dimension, began to speak its piece as I prepared my mid-morning coffee.

"You know," it said. "You should really take a look at those messages."

"I'm not interested in those messages," I said aloud pouring coffee from the pot into my coffee mug. I held the brown ceramic mug in my hands and put the opening of my nose close to the rim of the mug. The sweet aromas of beans from Columbia wafted into me, brightening my day just a bit. But I was interested in the messages.

I held off avoiding the opening of the 3 messages for as long as I could; they had been flashing red in the corner of my eye for the entire time I drank the dark Columbian coffee. Unafraid, I placed the mug into the sink and returned to the sofa I had collapsed upon last night.

I thought of the messages and casually glanced at the glass of detox my automatic maid had made for me upon registering from my vitals that I was awake. I couldn't have asked for a better time to realize the drink was there. I sat up as quick as a hare and gulped the drink. Feeling the cold liquid of the detox drip down my lips and neck, wetting the collar of the white button up I had worked and slept in from the day and night before. I minded not at all, allowing the feeling of being wet wrap around me. I need to take a shower, I thought to myself as the 1ˢᵗ of the messages appeared on the screen.

• ◆ •

It was from the Butterfly Man.

"Hey, Dr. Cane. I was wondering. Good morning by the way. I was wondering what it would take to schedule another session with you before the end of the week. I know it's Sunday and my next session isn't scheduled for another two weeks. But I was at a lost as to what to do about the neighbors and their nightly orgy parties. I'm sure that's what is happening over there. When I walk by their house they have neon lights going and an assortment of debaucherously sounding things coming forth from the windows. On occasion I have happened upon two or more individuals staggering out of the house and making their way towards god knows where. But the reason that I'm calling is because these have triggered my attention away from the enlightenment that I had in my hands. I need to see it again. Holding it in my hands is the only way I could ever again be able to bring meaning and understanding to everything. I'm free Thursday, anytime you are able to fit me in. Pretty please, Doctor Cane. I would greatly appreciate it."

The audio message ended. I was so thankful it wasn't a video message. I would have had to look at the sad display of the Butterfly Man, lamenting his woes upon me.

The Butterfly Man was an individual that had come to see me professionally for the first time just after the 4ᵗʰ upgrade of the implant. As his name paints him as, he was the portrait of a man covered in butterflies. When he first stepped into the office, I was overwhelmed with the flying insects. I saw the first one and thought, how odd it was for a monarch to be flapping its wings around and about. When my secretary came in to alert me of the Butterfly Man's presence, she let in a swarm of the recently cocooned bugs.

He walked in ahead, while leaving a trail behind him of butterflies. All different sorts of species seemed to take a liking to him and he didn't seem to mind much of their existence. Taking a seat in the place assigned for patients, the Butterfly Man bombarded his way into a session with me.

Waving off my secretary who was ready to call for the authorities I went about administering the preliminary test before beginning thought therapy, mainly because of the drugs given to the patient. It is of the utmost importance that the individual undergoing therapy be able to physically handle the drugs required to induce the proper state needed for the full effect of the therapy to work. If not, an overdose will occur without a doubt.

Above all, the butterfly wished to tell me of his plight with his wife. It seemed like such a trite thing to talk about, considering that I would have to over months peel away at him to understand. Butterflies were attracted to and attached themselves to the Butterfly Man. He was really a very simple person though, wanting only to live life as what he perceived as a normal human being. Asking for little, the Butterfly Man got his fair share of prejudice and discrimination.

The Butterfly Man began to release pheromones from his pores about around the time he reached puberty. From then as you can imagine his life was filled with difficulties. Unable to continue to attend school, the teachers and parents shunned him to exile and home school was all his parents were able to do for him. It didn't take long before the tension of such a freak of nature being their son, tore The Butterfly Man's mothers and father apart. Splitting ways, neither of them wanted anything to do with their freak of a son.

Cast into the orphanage system where far too few children are actually saved, the Butterfly Man was cast overboard in an angry sea.

Isolation and loneliness were the scars left to him by fates' perilous torment. Wishing upon countless stars and hoping beyond hope for a better tomorrow, the Butterfly Man found it when his section 8 approved of treatment in my facility.

Linking him up to the machine was the hardest thing. The drugs had a very strange effect on the butterflies too. They continued to stay on and around the Butterfly Man. But once he fell into the drug induced coma, the ones hanging on to his body, stopped flapping their wings. All the others swarming around him straightened into a single line that spiraled up and down the Butterfly Man like a barber shop candy cane.

Once inside of the Butterfly Man's mind, there were no insects to speak of. The entire experience presented to him and I as we walked through this mind was totally devoid of insects. This did not take away from the beauty of the scene, however.

There was much beauty. There was also a great deal of anger that manifested itself in the form of a raging bull that terrorized us the entire time we were inside of the Butterfly Man's mind. The bull prevented us from reaching the Butterfly Man's enlightenment. But from what he was able to see kept the Butterfly Man coming back for more thought therapy sessions. The drugs never hurt, either.

The 2nd message was from the woman whom the machines wouldn't work for.

The woman for whom machines wouldn't work for was none other than the great granddaughter of the original Grape Family that rescued the 50 states of America from being sold to the variety of dictators that had won their auction bids. She had been born into the last of the American royalties and therefore knew of life beyond the Company. She was of that rare breed of individual that knows they are special and unique and for no other reason than stubbornness, chooses to lay dormant these capabilities in preference to childish natures and other glib sort of things.

When we first met acquaintances, it was clear from the beginning that her parents, the acting heirs of the Grape fortune, had forced the then at the time 17-year-old woman into my office. She was 22 and eager to show her adulthood when she left me a message that morning.

"Doctor Cane, hello. Its Lucy Grape, of the Grape family," the voice on the recording began. How I loathed her insistence of stating her own importance.

"I'm not sure if you heard," she continued. "But there is a matter of grave importance that I must parlay with you, immediately. I know it's early, and your secretary told me that you wouldn't be in the office for another 4 hours, but now it's well into the afternoon and you are nowhere to be found. If I don't hear from you soon, I will be forced to deploy every manner available to me to find you. And find you I will."

This last part sounded very much like a threat.

"Anyway, hopefully you're good, doctor, Cane," the message ended. "I will wait a bit longer for your call, but I will put out a search for you if I don't hear from you soon."

The message from the woman whom machines wouldn't work for ended and I listened to and felt the silence of the kitchen I was in. I had been standing for some time after finishing my coffee and placing the mug into the sink. Contemplation flirting with me, coming into being, I shied away and returned my focus to the last message that had arrived for me.

The 3$^{rd}$ message was from Commander Bryant

"Doctor, Cane," the boisterous baritone rang from the phone message machines' speaker. "I trust you slept well. Perhaps you are still sleeping at this moment and that is why your phone went straight to voicemail." I glanced at the time the Commander had made his message. Sure enough, and glancing at the floating digital display positioned near the front door of the condo, I concluded that Commander Bryant was correct in his assumption.

"As I said that I'd call you tomorrow," the Commander continued. "It is now then. And there is still a great deal more that we need to discuss and go through. That's about all I can say on the phone.

Why don't we meet for dinner, sometime between the sun going down and the streetlights coming on? I know a great Martian restaurant we can try. I hope such things aren't too highbrow for you. There's just something about Martian chicken that I've been craving for all week. I'll send a car to pick you up just after the sun sets, that way you'll have ample time to leave whenever you want. As long as the sun hasn't set. Once again, I hate to remind you that failure to comply would be considered a threat upon the countries' national security and I could have you executed if I so deemed fit. But, we've only just begun the fun that I know we are going to have."

A very long moment passed where words seemed to vanish from both of our existences. Even sound itself seemed to be taking a leave of absence and the vacuum created repeated an echo of failure I tried hard to swallow and move on from.

After doing nothing for longer than I had wanted, I finally went about bathing, preparing a meal, doing my morning prayer (which I hadn't done for some time) and watching a few shows on television. The sun began to set. Glancing outside more frequently then I enjoy to admit, a car similar to the one I had driven in with the Commander, pulled up to the driveway of the condo I lived in. I scurried downstairs and set myself up comfortably into the plush leather seats. I buckled up and allowed myself to be whisked off and away to where I assumed would be the CSD headquarters. I was wrong in my assumption.

Pulling up to a house, after a drive longer than what I knew to be the distance to the CSD's main hub of operations. I observed a certain change in the environment, which got me suspicious of the area of which we were headed. Crackheads. That epidemic of addiction, none of which anyone would ever hope their child would have to endure. Cast from the light, these unmentionables never went farther than the nearest minstrel show; never before mentioned that which would not be seen in the days living sections.

A before mentioned individual met me and for the first time, I had the acquaintance to meet him.

"Doctor, Cane," Commander Bryant said. "This is Father Clementine."

We shook hands and I looked at the man I had never known before this meeting.

◆ ◆ ◆

The thought therapy sessions of Vladimir Fortune had lasted for some months. Not a long time in terms of the set aside recommendations of treatment. However, the months that did pass were enough to assist Commander Bryant. He was most cunning. There, I had revealed something with which wasn't what we wanted. Now who is this, you should be asking. And yes it is you, the one that happens to be reading this abysmal attempt at presenting myself to you. How it happened, to whom and where. It is this we had hoped you'd not notice.

◆ ◆ ◆

Take with a promise that we shall return to what I alluded to. As to where it all was taking place. Father Clementine was to lead us both, Commander Bryant and I, Doctor Cane, to the promised land of a wealthy parlay. Nothing of the sort happened and we were lost at sea, as it were. Left to the imaginations of many, death seemed as suitable of a definition to set upon the likes of us. We shall forgive them for their folly. But digressions alone, there wasn't a single one that gave to me a chance at breath, that should hope to equal what the Commander did for me. Before I killed him. And kill him I did.

After the introductions and learning that Father Clementine wasn't of a pious nature at all, I threw myself at his feet and the uncharacteristic nature of me took over. Here I was, a Buddhist kissing a Catholic's feet, for fear of the reprimand I knew was coming. If I didn't stay in line, like a good nigga should…that's getting too far off from our story so I digress.

• ◆ •

It seemed Commander Bryant wasn't the only one profoundly interested in Vladimir Fortune's memories of all the past lives the entity could remember.

It didn't take long to see that Father Clementine wasn't without his tactical strengths. Generally, he was a bad motha-fucka. But specifically, he was an educated and moderate individual that would help any fellow man, regardless of whether or not they were for or against the cloth.

"Now, I believe it is time, Doctor Cane," Father Clementine began to say as we sat in the large backyard of the most luxurious house I had ever had the pleasure of stepping foot in. "For you to be fully read in to the dealings we are engaged in. As Commander Bryant has made you slightly aware, citizens of the United Companies of America, are unknowingly engaged in a blood pact with the Fire Demon, Ahka. This is by order of the Tribunal and there isn't anything either you or I can do about that. We serve this Fire Demon, Ahka, and we are bound to it. The entity formally known as, Vladimir Fortune, has a particularly strong life force that Ahka has grown famished for. We were close to apprehending the entity, as you know. However, because of the incompetence of some of our best agents, we were unsuccessful in making an arrest."

I scuffed at the pleasant way Father Clementine was saying they had murdered Vladimir. The way it was described to me by Commander Bryant, before making the acquaintance of Father Clementine and learning all that I told you of earlier, Vlad's untimely demise was horrific beyond measured degree.

"As the Commander has already explained to you," Father Clementine continued. "Your firsthand knowledge of the entity, and most importantly your thought therapy records with Vladimir Fortune, will be an invaluable help to us."

"Yes, he's explained this to me. I haven't decided, however, if I am to agree with helping you," I said draining my 2nd bottle of beer. A servant hastily presented another before me. I raised an eyebrow and glanced down at the freshly opened beverage, foam hovering along the rim.

"Yes, we figured you'd say something along those lines. I hope we don't have to remember that our, requesting, of your services is merely a courtesy we offer to individuals the Tribunal holds in the highest respects. I assure you, if you take their kindness as weakness, you will surely be thrown under a bus you would never see coming," Father Clementine said squaring his jaw and centering his eyes on my own. "Please take your time in considering," he said taking his eyes off of mine, leaning back in the lawn chair he sat in and stared at the dome overhead.

I took my time and considered.

What on earth had I gotten myself into? I asked myself. Finding that I was staring at the massive garden tucked away in the far end of the large lawn that seemed to expand the length of an entire football field, I saw the image of Sifu Ping pop into being. It's usually for some alarming reason that my teacher appears. Never knowing if it truly will be the last time I see him, I always make an effort to focus my attention on the subtle lesson I know is lurking somewhere within the visit.

Bee's buzzed loops around Sifu Ping's head and he stood unblinking, staring at me. Commander Bryant nor Father Clementine could see my old teacher. He only continued to live within me. This was of course before the Crimson Knight cut the last of his remaining life force that had gone on living within me, in half. Just before you all placed me here, in this cage.

"Come now, Doctor Cane," Father Clementine said, his patience seeming to have run its length. "It really doesn't take that much consideration."

I had to admit unfortunately, that he was right.

"Are you a real priest?" I asked arbitrarily making an attempt to stall for time. My attempt at reclaiming some semblance of dignity, I suppose.

Father Clementine indulged me. "Born and bred," he answered. "My family were Catholics even in the old world, before the Companies owned the land.

"Ah, I see. So, you're working for the Tribunal out of a religious obligation, or some such thing?"

"There is more of a blood oath that has been made, by my great grandfather before me. Locking me by the marrow of my bone, to this land we stand upon."

"How unlucky for you," I said to Father Clementine sighing for a moment honestly for his own sake.

"You, too, are about to join us, Doctor Cane," Father Clementine said, as if on command. I'm sure he probably was. Commander Bryant produced a scalpel and presented it to me. Next to me, Father Clementine slowly slid a gold coin with the UCA symbol upon it. A terrifying Bear-Wolf. "From now we enter a pact," Father Clementine began to utter the words we citizens of the UCA have had engrained into our veins since the time we are first cast into the Tribunal's public-school curriculum. The acceptance into a system that once in, the only way out is upon death. My mother had strictly admonished me never to be a part of such a system. Here I was being forced to enter without a choice.

I grabbed the scalpel, sliced my thumb and put my bloody print upon the Bear-Wolf's face. The Commander collected it and placed the coin into a small piece of plastic similar to the one of sprinkles he had handed me the day before.

"Don't worry, there's more," the Commander said winking at me.

"Yes, lots more," Father Clementine chimed in. "Now that the pact has been made, we can speak more freely. And you can move about this country with an ease you'll never have known the likes of. Trust me on the heights to which you are about to soar, Doctor Cane. How I envy your virginity."

I nodded and smiled shyly, quite unsure how to take Father Clementine's speech. After all, he was a man of the cloth.

The problem asserted itself quickly as the Father was required to take his leave of Commander Bryant and I. Giving the proper salutes and salutations, Father Clementine dashed away to the car waiting for him in the front entrance of the Commander's large home. For a time, I sat pondering deeply. The Commander, having left to escort Father Clementine to the front door, took his time returning to the backyard where I sat, continuing to take sips of the alcohol being served to me by the robotic maid.

Sifu Ping, having stood the entire time in the same spot by the large garden in the back of the expansive yard, walked from his position and took a seat next to me. He crossed his legs and looked at the spot that he had been standing in all this time. The sun had begun to set and the soft orange glow bouncing off of the suns retreat painted Commander Bryant's Spanish style backyard into a gloss of melancholy.

"Do you have a cigarette?" Sifu Ping asked me, finally turning his head to face me.

"You know I don't have a cigarette," I responded.

"Eck, you never have the things on you that you need when you need 'em," my teacher said removing a pack of squares from the breast pocket of his light cotton jacket he wore. He tapped the top of the pack a few times and then placed one between his lips.

"Are those even real?" I asked him as he slid his middle finger against the wooden picnic table we rested our arms upon. A spark ignited and a flame omitted from the tip of Sifu Ping's middle finger. As he lit his square it looked as if he were flipping me off.

"They're as real as anything in whatever the hell you would call this reality I'm existing in. It isn't living that's for sure," Sifu Ping said taking a few quick drags from the square before shaking his hand free of the flame.

"We're going to have ahold of the tablets," I finally said to my teacher, stating that which I hadn't wanted to admit.

Sifu Ping smoked and nodded his head.

"Yes," he said. "As far as I know, they now currently only exist in your brain. Isn't this correct?"

"Yes, it is," I responded nodding my head up and down.

"You remember what happened the last time you started being your own guide during thought therapy sessions into your own mind," Sifu Ping said snubbing the cigarette onto the wooden picnic table.

I looked with alarm for a moment forgetting that my teacher only existed in my thoughts. Thanks to a last-ditch charm that he had held deep in his heart, and an agreement on my part, Sifu Ping's essence was able to live on within me. I absorbed his knowledge and abilities, while the essence of my teacher retained his wisdom. The arrangement served, until he was killed by the Crimson Knight, a great deal of value to my life and those around me.

"You don't have to remind me about that," I said to my teacher beginning to grow irritated at the memory he had conjured up of my dark times as a thought therapist. "I won't be falling back into that place again, you don't have to worry about that," I vehemently responded.

"You never had intended to end up there in the first place. You were seduced in and then trapped.

"Why do you insist on reliving these things?" I asked trying to rid myself of my teacher, for now.

At just that moment, the Commander finally returned from his overlong absence.

"We're going to have to find the tablet of Vladimir Fortune's memory inside of my own," I said to him before he could even sit down."

"We need to what?" he asked furrowing his brow and retaking his seat.

The tablet. I've seen it, many times. It became something of a fascination for the both of us," I continued rambling faster than I was making sense.

"What is this Tablet?" Commander Bryant asked of me. Sifu Ping shaking his head, popped out of the pictures screen I had been viewing him in. Commander Bryant noticed me staring at the empty air as if someone was there and asked if I were ok.

Shaking my head clear, I responded that I was ok and continued on with my explanation of what the tablets were.

"Everyone's thoughts and actions are engraved on a giant slab of warm marble by the two record keepers – Same Birth and Same Name – that reside in a realm in our minds called the Karmic Repository."

"The Karmic Repository?" Commander Bryant asked squinting his eyes in puzzlement.

"Yes, where all of your good and bad thoughts and actions are stored," I said.

"But who is it stored for? Who is the one that reads and judges the end results of all the good and bad that's been done?"

I was impressed at the Commander's insight. He had touched on questions none in the thought therapy profession had thus found been able to discover an answer to. "That, Commander Bryant," I truthfully answered him. "That is a question that is at the very heart of Thought Therapy. I have no answer for you, I am afraid to say. But I do know that such a tablet exists in every individual, just as every person has an enlightenment to grasp floating somewhere within them."

"And you've seen Vladimir's tablet?" Commander Bryant asked not missing a beat.

"Yes, I have," I responded feeling the electricity of a crazy idea beginning to sizzle. "I've viewed almost the entirety of the damn thing, beyond his own enlightenment. Vlad wanted nothing more than to read through his own tablet. I had never seen anything quite like it, as a matter of fact. Most people become addicted to possessing their enlightenment. For Vladimir, however, reading off the tablet enamored him."

"Why do you think that is?" the commander asked taking a sip of whiskey that the servant robotic maid placed before us both.

I could feel the liquor begin to take its full effect upon me. I had been sitting there in the Commander's backyard drinking at the wooden picnic table for some time. The orange glow faded away and was replaced by the black dark of a cloudy sky.

"I think he was remembering his memories of past lives. Doubling down on their record. Each character was engraved in the thickest of carvings I have ever seen in all my years of thought therapy," I explained a little bit more animatedly than I had intended. The effect didn't go unnoticed by the Commander however.

"Doubling down on his memories?" Commander Bryant asked to no one in particular. Rubbing the stubble on his chin, he drained the glass of whiskey he had been nursing while in deep contemplation. "So, we're going to have to go into your brain if we wish to see Vladimir Fortune's tablet then," he stated as a matter of fact.

I nodded my head in consent and drained my own glass of whiskey. The burn felt good. Much better than the very real fear that I knew was preparing to be thrust upon me. The Commander asked the correct question.

"Have you ever yourself gone through thought therapy?"

I nodded my head that I had. It was customary that I did once or twice a year. Twice was the recommended treatment for licensed practicing thought therapy physicians to go through thought therapy with an approved therapist as a guide. There have been known cases of some thought therapist developing a split within their psyche and creating an alternate self that accompanies the therapist when they go in as a guide into their patient's minds. When such a split occurs, it almost always originates in a portion of the self reserved for fundamental evil. That evil which exist within every human being.

"What we're talking about," I finally spoke up. "Is a bit different, however. It's also a lot more dangerous, for the both of us."

Commander Bryant looked at me and that damn smile reappeared on his face. "I'm glad you're not fighting the pact you made?" he said abruptly changing topics.

"You all have my blood," I said. "Why would I?"

"You know, you'd be very surprised," the Commander said. "I've seen very noble men and women beg to be released from the pacts they made with the Tribunal."

"And you?" I asked the Commander.

"What of me?" Commander Bryant asked.

"What pact did you enter?" I clarified my question.

"I am like Father Clementine," he said.

"How so?"

"The Admiral signed my life away to service of the Tribunal. He knew the truth just as all eventually find. There is no resisting their will. You are about to learn how great the rewards are to those that are under a blood pact with the Tribunal, though. They do at least make up for taking one's soul."

The casual nature with which the Commander was talking caused goosebumps to break across every inch of my skin, as the temperature seemed to drop in great degrees around me. The moon had begun to make its appearance with its bright hues reflecting white illumination down from its full form. Commander Bryant slapped his hand on the wooden picnic table and announced that that was that and the night was ready to be brought to an end.

I shook hands with the Commander and bid him adieu.

"This car will take you home," the Commander said pointing to a sedan with the backseat door being held open by a beautiful young brown-skinned woman dressed in a fitted tuxedo. This will be your personal car and driver from now on.

I heard the Commander's words but the drink had clogged my ears and I paid no attention to this comment, until the next morning when the same woman was standing outside of the front entrance of my condo, waiting for me with the back door of the same sedan open.

Commander Bryant helped me into the car and closed the door. I lowered the back window and glanced out at the commander who was still standing by the door.

"If you need anything," he started. "Please under no circumstances do you need to hesitate to ask. We are here to serve you now, doctor. As long as you assist us to the best of your ability, of course."

"Of course," I repeated aloud. More to myself than Commander Bryant. "The only thing I need help with are my dreams," I casually said trying to make a quip.

"What do you mean?" the Commander asked taking a bit of interest.

I shouldn't have opened my mouth, I thought looking down at the leather floor rug my feet were resting upon in the luxury sedan. Commander Bryant's eyes pulled my own back to his and I could feel his smile beginning to creak its way onto his lips.

"I had a dream about the Crimson Knight," I blurted out not wanting to see that smile again.

"Why didn't you say something earlier about this?" Commander Bryant asked with what appeared to be genuine alarm smacked across his face.

"I wasn't sure it was relevant," I lied.

"Doctor Cane, I know this is all a little outside of your frame of reference. But I must remind you that when we say national security depends upon your complete cooperation, we really mean it."

I wasn't sure but it was beginning to seem like Commander Bryant was becoming angry with me.

"I'm sorry, sir," I said for lack of anything better to say. "I'm not quite sure how my dreams have any basis on the investigation you are currently involved in."

"We, Doctor Cane. The investigation we are involved in. The gold coin with your blood on it has joined the pot of so many other hundreds of millions just like it," the Commander reminded me. Not that he needed to.

"All to serve the Fire Demon?" I sarcastically asked.

"No," the Commander sardonically responded. "You serve the Tribunal, just as I do. And we have been tasked with destroying the Fire Demon. Or at least severing its hold upon us that we were bamboozled into falling under."

"You mean the Tribunal," I said.

"Now now, Doctor Cane. Do be careful. One must never forget oneself and the surroundings with which they live. Such statements, as I'm sure you are fully aware, cannot be made and go unpunished."

"Threats?" I asked feeling my stomach boil in disgust at the audacity of these people. Yet I was quickly informed how much of an ant I truly was by the Commander.

"Doctor Cane, these are no threats. As long as you are standing on this land with an implant, you and I will do what the Tribunal tells us to. Now, as to your visit from the Crimson Knight, I'm afraid I will have to be forced to provide you with a security detail."

"Excuse me?" I asked unsure of what I thought I heard the Commander say.

"We are going to have to assign you a security perimeter," Commander Bryant patiently said.

"What will that consist of?" I asked with anger preparing to explode from my belly which it had been boiling in all this time.

"A security perimeter will consist of 4-5 shadows that will be charged with protecting your life, Doctor Cane," Commander Bryant said.

"Do you really think all of that is necessary?" I asked dumbfounded.

"Doctor Cane?" the Commander asked glancing at me hard from the corner of his eye. "We don't exactly know who the hell the Crimson Knight is. So yes, it is absolutely necessary that you are assigned a perimeter of shadows." That damn grin of Commander Bryant's wasn't far behind after he said this.

Just then, his phone began to ring. The Commander picked it up and I tried to continue thinking about what he had just said, the weight of it all. And at the same time, I tried to pretend that I wasn't interested in whom he was talking to on the phone. The Commander, as if reading my mind, put the call on speaker and let me listen. The voice of Father Clementine, still fresh in my mind sounded from somewhere in the throat of the Commander.

"We will be watching your progress with a concerned eye, yes?" the Tribunal head lap dog, Father Clementine, said to Commander Bryant.

"Good," he responded. "I'm glad you're watching."

The call ended.

"Well, goodnight then, Doctor Cane," the Commander said tapping the back of his ear and I imagine shuffling through any other phone messages he had. I nodded my head and made to enter the back seat of the luxury sedan Commander Bryant was still holding the door open to. A thought quickly brought me back. "Yes?" he asked me.

"You never told me what Rah Pooh was?" I asked immediately regretting that I had done so when I saw the Commanders smile return to his lips.

"Rah Pooh is a person," Commander Bryant said closing his eyes. "He's a person from my past. When I was still a cadet and hiding out in the uncharted areas of the basic boot camp, Rah Pooh was the only other kid I was able to get along with. I think it was more he got along with me, really. He was from an unmarked island out near Laos. Real quiet. Strong as hell and had these eyes that were like daggers into the heart."

"You were in love with him?" I asked picking up on the hint.

"I was, very much indeed. You could say he was my boyfriend. When we were out there living in the trees, those were the greatest most liberating years of my life. Left to be me. I'm sure the Admiral knew about it. The Admiral seemed to know everything. But such things were irrelevant to him, as far as his frame of reality was concerned. I don't very well believe I would have survived this period of my life had it not been for Rah Pooh. He was wiser than me, even though I had two years of life on him. Age was nothing but a number with us, though."

An Aaliyah track of the same name popped into the background noise of my thoughts, as I listened to Commander Bryant reveal a defining moment of his life to me.

"The two of us kept each other warm at night, and during the day we explored and discovered the uncharted terrain. Because of my adventures in the outskirts with the Admiral, beyond the rim—not to mention, I had a great deal of outdoor survival knowledge because of Rah Pooh and where he grew up, wherever that was—the land we were trekking through seemed like a cake walk, judging from what he told me during nights, cuddling."

"So why was his name being chanted in your mind?" I asked sensing the ending of this love story was very tragic.

"That was his voice chanting," the Commander replied.

"He was chanting his own name?" I asked wondering.

"Yes," Commander Bryant answered, saying nothing else afterwards.

Silence, that bitch of a friend, dipped in and took its time in leaving.

"What happened?" I finally asked unable to hold myself back any longer.

The Commander looked at me and let out a long painful exhalation.

"Around about the time we were entering our junior exams. I didn't take them but Rah Pooh insisted upon his participation in nothing else but the exams, for reasons I never was able to ascertain. While we were preparing dinner over an open fire, a Bear-Wolf got the jump on us. I didn't hear it, and Rah Pooh with his almost 6th sense with animals, mutated and normal alike, heard not a peep. In the quickest motion I've ever seen, the Bear-Wolf lopped off my young lover Rah Pooh's head, cleanly. There was a brief pause where time stood frozen. Even the Bear-Wolf seemed to appreciate the moment ensuing. During this pause in reality, that is when I saw for the first and last time the Pink Fluffy Bunny."

"The ferryman for souls going to the afterlife?" I asked taken aback at the turn in the story.

"Yes," he calmly responded to me. The very entity.

"What happened?" I asked leaning on the door now along with the Commander, staring into his eyes, transfixed on his answer.

"I watched as my friend Rah Pooh's soul was taken away from me. Once he and the bunny faded into nothing, I slayed the Bear-Wolf. As I had done many times at that point. I never entered my Senior Year after that. When the Admiral came and collected me, we immediately flew out of the UCA. Like I said, I'm sure the Admiral knew everything. I saw a therapist and got my mind together and after a few months was deemed clear and sane. Then the Admiral told me that I was to start my career in the CSD, the only acting force of military and law enforcement inside the borders of this wonderful country of ours," Commander Bryant said adding the ending to enlighten the Tribunal agents undoubtedly listening.

The Tribunal had a direct line in to each and every citizen with an implant, which was anyone within the borders of the United Companies of America. Born and bred, we were the controlled society existing in the otherwise free world.

My curiosity having been sedated, I made my leave of Commander Bryant and returned home via the car that was to be mine indefinitely, now that I was a part of something 'greater.'

# Chapter Six:

## Master Your Mind

About two days or so later…

*Horace Silver's 'Tokyo Blues,'* was playing from the condo below mine, as I began to go over my thought therapy session notes with Vladimir Fortune. The couple under me were a pair of artists that had ungodly work hours, but they played nice music and we always got along fine. Minding not the faint melody creaking from beneath the floorboards, I admired the large pile of boxes, all filled with paper and recordings. I hadn't noticed until that moment, but Vlad was the patient I had collected the most data on. The one I had obsessed the most over, I supposed, as I knelt down and began to rummage through a box containing what seemed to be a random stack of notes.

I didn't know what exactly the Tribunal was looking for, but I did know information concerning the Crimson Knight was probably the top on their priority list. I had already kept that separated in a box titled important so that was easy enough to come by. It was the task of compiling the rest of the data I had gathered that I knew was going to be a large project. I didn't know it was going to take me the better part of four years though. My blood pact with the Tribunal insured me a salary beyond the likes I would never have been able to obtain, chipping away at my practice one patient at a time as I were, before cutting my finger before Father Clementine.

Flipping through loose pages of notes comprising the years of thought therapy with Vladimir Fortune, I once again lost myself in research. The pursuit of what I fell in love with in the first place returned to me. I've never been able to describe the feeling of ruffling through pages of recorded memory, learning the patterns of the universe. Held within each and every patient are puzzles, unlocking for every thought therapist the things which they themselves fundamentally question.

Probing the boundaries of sanity and crossing over into an observational realm that is the transition point of madness, I rifled through files and fell into my mind. Sifu Ping kept me company the week it took to spread out and analyze the archive. The work was therapeutic and helped me get back to the level of sprinkle balance needed to exist as a thought therapist. Abuse of sprinkles is the quickest way to lose one's license in the difficult world of thought therapy. It takes so much to even get a license, that to lose one would be gravely stupid.

As I read my summaries and listened to our talking sessions— the talking sessions always must take place before the actual diving into the patient's mind can occur—I began to come to terms with a lot of things. I knew what I was and I knew who I was, but I did not know what I was doing.

I hadn't dug up my archives since I had begun my practice of thought therapy. Sifu Ping stood in the corner and watched while I searched for what I did not know existed.

How do I know this is even legit, I thought to myself beginning to feel dumb after coming to a session summary around the time just before Vlad stopped his own sessions. His reasons were cryptic and I assumed he was moving on to a different Company. Thought therapy isn't something one should be doing for longer than a few years. Chemically the body isn't able to handle the drugs patients are given to induce the comatose state required to descend to the correct league they are under. At the point just before Vlad stopped therapy, we had been discussing at length about his childhood in the current life Vlad had been living.

Over the course of the previous 2 to 3 years before this point, Vlad told me his memories from each of his past lives, chronologically. I've already relayed some of that earlier to you and was unable to find anything more that would be worth telling you. What was of interest, and not a moment too soon for I was leading myself directly into the loony bin searching through all that data, was Vlad's relations with Niki Brown while they were in school.

As far as I know from the collection of summaries of thought therapy sessions and the tapes of our pre-therapy session, Niki Brown was the only person that was able to give Vlad the desire to not continue remembering his past lives. So dearly did he love this woman, as I read through the summary of the walk in his mind, the projection of her showed up as we were exploring another set of stairs leading to unknown dimensions in Vlad's mind.

Vladimir had so many stairs leading to other places. More than any other thought therapy patient ever recorded. Over the years I was Vlad's therapist, I became something of a celebrity for the papers I wrote based off of the discoveries I was able to come across in Vlad's brain. The overlaying of memories on his psyche created a mirror within a mirror effect, rippling what seemed to be an infinite worth of differing possible worlds one could fall into. Being Vlad's guide was something of a joke I broke to him quite early on immediately following our first thought therapy session.

"Vlad, there's something I must admit to you," I said to him as we stood in the loading room for the 2nd time.

"What's up, Doctor Cane?" he asked me looking sincere as he always did.

"Well, to be direct about it, I'm not going to be an effective guide I think for your journeys into your mind. There's just too much that I can't place. Too many things I've never seen. A lot of things I don't think I could even imagine. Just that first visit was more than I could handle. Over the last week since then, I've been researching through every journal and study available to try and explain the things we saw. I was able to learn some things, but I'm afraid now, we really are heading into uncharted territory. I'm afraid danger may very well lurk at the bottom of the next staircase we climb down."

I let myself register what I had just said and shook my head internally, as I had just violated the oath of thought therapy. But honesty seemed to be best, given the severity of what could go wrong if something did. We both could die. Or worse, be stuck in Vladimir's mind until my secretary discovered us. Then we would be disconnected and if we didn't die, we'd be forever vegetables floating in whatever stream of consciousness we were lucky enough to fall into. Hopefully not the sunken place.

"That's ok doc," Vlad said smiling. "I'm just happy to see what's inside. When you remember as many lives as I have, there isn't much that's taken with a whole lot of weight. I've been born, grown up, developed and tried to live a decent enough life and died, many times over. Remembering it all often makes me feel older than my current life, hundreds of years older in fact. So for this reason, I am not afraid of what is in my mind," Vladimir said pride oozing from his chest.

The loading room became ready and with that we were off down the stairs for our second, of a great many, thought therapy session.

We would soon learn, however, that it's what was trying to get inside of Vlad's mind that was the most terrifying of all. The Crimson Knight made his first official appearance into our thought therapy sessions a little after the first year. Terrified doesn't do justice to what I felt the first time I saw the crisscrossed and loopy-loop highways of fire.

The Crimson Knight rode in the far distance and in a blink, he was upon Vlad and me.

His hot breath bouncing against my face and the heat of the flames singeing me. I stood petrified by the Crimson Knights telepathic powers. I knew from the feel of the world that somehow we had been pulled out of Vlad's mind and transported to a realm outside of the physical reality existing in the world that I am sitting in, here in this cell, desperately writing these last words to you before they put the noose around my neck.

Vlad and I were frozen in place where we stood, watched by the Crimson Knight intimately stalking us, only my eyes darting from side-to-side. Little good it did me though. Just as suddenly as it all began; we were back inside of Vlad's mind and came to reality in the loading room. My watch sounded off the hour mark and we returned to the waking world.

"Was that the Crimson Knight?" I asked Vlad as I helped him groggily arise from his drug-induced coma.

"Yes, that was the Crimson Knight," he answered exhausted.

"What did he want?" I asked trying to shake the heat that I still seemed to feel coercing against my skin.

"I don't know what he wants," Vlad responded. "He's only just sniffed me out. It's nice you were able to see it too though. I honestly thought it was an indication that I was me losing my mind.

"No," I shook my head. "Vlad, if there's one thing that isn't happening, it's that you're losing your mind. Honestly, I'm shocked you haven't fallen completely insane already, which attests to the strength of your spirit more than anything."

"This time it's very different though," Vlad said. "I can't quite put my finger on it."

"You mean when we were ambushed by the Crimson Knight?" I asked.

"No, what I mean is being in this life. This body. There's always been a different feeling about it."

"Like how do you mean?" I asked seeing the annoyance begin to highlight upon his face.

"My entire life I've never been able to really articulate it. But I'd say it's the feelings. I feel more in this life than I ever remember doing in any other life," Vlad said to me.

"What do you mean by feeling?"

"What I mean is. Like, people around me, I can feel their emotions," Vlad answered thinking hard and choosing his words carefully.

"You mean empathize? You're able to empathize with those around you?"

"No, it's way more than just that. I've always been able to literally feel other people's emotions. And once they get inside of me they fight with my own emotions for control of which ones I feel. Neither of them ever win the battle and I'm left feeling like shit," Vlad said, his voice beginning to tremble.

"Yes, I can understand what you mean," I responded trying my best to put together a hypothesis of what Vlad was doing his best to describe. "It could be that the body you were born into, this being that is you, for the moment, has a highly attuned sense of empathy. You're an empath," I said as professionally of a doctor sounding voice I could muster. The fact of the matter was, when it came to Vlad, I had no idea where to begin.

◆

"Why didn't you tell the Commander you knew about the Fire Demon? The Tribunal made a pact with you," Sifu Ping asked me from the memories I swam through that were being pulled up from the data I reviewed.

"What'd you say?" I asked the image of my teacher whose last remaining essence existed within me.

"The Fire Demon," Sifu Ping repeated. "When the Commander and Father Clementine were talking about it, you acted as if you had never heard the name before. Why?"

"It was you that taught me never to reveal any information for free," I responded rising from the ground where I had been going through all the back files from the thought therapy sessions with Vladimir Fortune. My knees cracked and the age that had begun to deteriorate away my status as a young man peaked its painful head above the ground where I tried my best to keep it buried.

I suppose it's the Tribunal that's going to beat age in the contest to bring my life to an end.

"Was I supposed to reveal that I knew what they were talking about?" I asked indignation brushing off of the tip of my tongue.

Sifu Ping shook his head. "No, I didn't say that," he said. "But entering into a blood pact with the Tribunal, and now you're connected to the Fire Demon we worked so hard to banish from this planet."

"It was the only way," I said, not sure if that was even true. I hadn't seen any other way, but they had ambushed me with making the pact. There wasn't much choice I had and Sifu Ping knew that. "The Tribunal runs the Companies and all those that are citizens of them. With these things in our heads," I said tapping the implant sewn into the back of my ear. "There isn't much that can be done to resist them."

My teacher nodded his head in reluctant agreement. "Yea, I know" he said. You know what this means now don't you?"

"Yes, I do," I responded sober and with a sigh.

"It's going to have to die this time. Do you still have the diamond scalpel we used the first time to sever his connection to Earth?" Sifu Ping asked me. We had migrated to the couch and I was drinking a beer I had grabbed from the fridge.

"Yea, I still have it. I sewed it into my thigh before I left China."

"You've been walking around with the Diamond Scalpel in your leg since we battled the Fire Demon?" Sifu Ping asked, surprised.

"You said to keep it safe," I responded. "And after all that we had to go through to collect the damn materials to make it, I couldn't think of a better place."

"Doesn't it cut you?" my teacher asked with a hint of concern sneaking away from his voice.

I moved my chin to my left shoulder and stared into the eyes of the man living inside my imagination. "Every time I walk," I responded after allowing silence to have its moment.

The image of Sifu Ping, that only I could see, shuddered. "Well, looks like you're going to have to cut that out," he said to me rising to his feet.

"Where are you off to?" I asked

"To get some rest," he replied. "I have a feeling this is going to be the deciding battle for both of our lives. I want to be ready."

This alarmed me. I had never known Sifu Ping not to be ready. He didn't allow me time to question him, however, as my teacher popped up and went wherever it is deep into my essence, where I couldn't access him.

I sat staring at the space where he had just been standing, or where I was imagining him standing. When the phone began to ring. I pushed the implant behind my ear and a video screen popped up in my eyeball's vision. It was Commander Bryant.

"Doctor Cane," he said in greeting. "I hope that your research has been promising."

"I've come across a few leads, mainly concerning this Fire Demon. I had some more questions about it."

"So, you have come across Ahka, the Fire Demon," Commander Bryant said, that damn all-knowing smile beginning to spread over his lips. "We figured you had and all you needed was a little jarring of your memory with data."

"Well, you all were correct," I said thinking how I would have liked to punch the Commander right in his chiseled face at that moment.

I imagined him countering my attack and pummeling me into an embarrassing submission that I just might wake up in the hospital from.

"That's great news," Commander Bryant said, urgency arriving in his tone. "Unfortunately, some things have occurred and we require your expertise."

` "Oh," I said. "What's going on?"

"I'll brief you in the car," the Commander said. "I'm downstairs."

"But of course you are," I said, not meaning to say aloud.

"We're going to have a lot of fun hunting the entity formally known as Vladimir Fortune and the Fire Demon known as Ahka" Commander Bryant said. "You don't need to bring anything. Let's go." The call canceled.

I looked around my condo at the scattered piles of data, in its different forms, and felt the walls beginning to close in on me. I needed to go outside. Grabbing a jacket, I left everything as it was and headed downstairs to the car Commander Bryant was waiting in it.

"I hope you're ready for the real fun, because it is about to begin," the Commander said as I hopped into the sedan, shut the door and rode off to the CSD headquarters. I was informed by the Commander once we hit the expressway that we'd be meeting the doctor this evening.

"Who's the doctor?" I asked very confused and trying my best to erase the feelings of emptiness arising from my search through the past.

When I first met the doctor that invented the machine allowing data stored in implants to be replayed, Sifu Ping immediately informed me that the doctor had been a student of his.

"You were a student of Sifu Ping," I said to him as we shook hands after Commander Bryant introduced us.

He looked at me, eyes widened in shock. "How did you know that?' he asked me.

"Sifu Ping says that there is no time that will ever repeat more than those that are regretted when we lay down to sleep," I said to him repeating the sentence Sifu Ping told me to say.

The doctor that invented the machine continued to stare at me. He had that look of how did I know, but he knew how I knew, on his face. There was no mistaking the fact that we had both been through Sifu Ping University.

Sifu Ping University was the most cutthroat, no holds barred, sink or swim cruel tutelage one could ever embark upon. Naturally, none knew how devastating instruction under Sifu Ping would be. One of the first rules was secrecy. There was no talking about what went on in China. I doubt I could write anything of accuracy to you reading these pages, concerning the reality of this all.

◆ ◆ ◆

"It's come time for us to slay the Crimson Knight, has it?" the doctor said to me closing his eyes and nodding his head.

"I guess so," I said.

"So you did know of the Crimson Knight?" Commander Bryant asked me smiling.

"You already knew that," I responded.

"Indeed I did, Doctor Cane. We all have known that," the Commander said tapping the implant in the back of his ear.

Of course I thought. The Tribunal knows everything, including our thoughts.

"What I don't understand," I said beginning to accept the stance of the fact that the jig was up. "Why this whole game? Why waste all this time? Why get me locked into this blood pact?"

The Commander laughed. Doctor Cane, the Tribunal can read your thoughts, but they cannot know which direction they will go. Therefore, it was necessary to use your analytical skills in order to get the information we needed. The information which you are going to provide for us, now!"

That damn smile told me all I needed to know. I felt my shoulders sag in resignation. They just wanted me into the blood pact, I thought to myself as I watched the doctor and Commander Bryant exchange knowing glances. But why? I could not understand. Sifu Ping watched me from the door of the Commander's office.

That very door opened as I stared feeling my entire world engulf my heart in a sadness I thought I had overcome. There seemed to be no limit to how far down I was falling. Even though I stood there in the office and watched as Father Clementine walked through, there was nothing I could do about the sinking taking place inside of me. My stomach sucked inward and I wasn't able to breathe. I collapsed to my knees and then began to realize what had occurred. The passage of time became a stranger.

When did time become an unknown entity to me? When did it become so hard to know what the time of day felt like? It feels like morning, yet it's darker than a dank cave. When it feels like night, the sun is brilliantly shinning its luminous nurturing light. I didn't know what was going on, but I knew I could no longer trust my senses.

Maybe it was the drugs the Commander gave me. No, I thought to myself, he wasn't out to get me. I had been inside of his mind; I knew what he was about. Commander Bryant was all service and duty. Loyalty was something he adhered to more than anything. That was why he continued to stay married to his wife, because she wanted it. He had wronged her and he knew it. Yet the reasons were his own, locked away in a place even I wasn't privy too.

"You mustn't fight it, Doctor Cane," Father Clementine said to me walking toward where I knelt. "There isn't anything you could have done to avoid the inevitability of this situation. We have all that we need from you, and what a great help you've been to the Tribunal. A life of security and riches beyond those you could ever dream are guaranteed to you. You've served the Tribunal well."

My vision blurred as Father Clementine put his hand on my shoulder and shoved me backwards onto the carpeted floor of Commander Bryant's office. As gravity pulled my weight down, an element seeming to betray me, slowed beyond my own heartbeat. My thoughts raced. It took a long time for me to feel and realize I was laid out flat on my back, staring up at the three on the clock.

"What do we do with him?" I heard the doctor ask Commander Bryant and Father Clementine. I was blacking out and the screen of my vision slowly narrowed to a single scope of what I could see. I was falling into myself.

When I woke I was in the loading room. Well this isn't good, I thought to myself. *Stevie Wonder's 'Songs in the Key of Life,'* could be heard. The album had been playing for some time. I'm not sure how I knew this, but I did. When I rose to my feet in the loading room, *'Sir Duke'* was playing from the invisible overhead speakers. This was my thought therapy soundtrack, but who was to be my guide, I wondered as I waited for the moment to arrive.

Commander Bryant popped into the loading room as *Stevie Wonder's 'I Wish'* came to an end.

He stood before me with that all-knowing, frustration inducing smile. I wanted to rip it off of his face.

Sifu Ping popped into vision right behind him. I heard him in my head and he explained to me what was about to take place.


"The machine doctor's diamond scalpel, used to remove the implant, and the diamond scalpel sewn into your leg, together must be used. One to destroy the Crimson Knight and the other to destroy the Fire Demon. Both must have their eyes removed and eaten. Only then can the great pure evil that is the Fire Demon be destroyed."


*'Knock Me Off My Feet'* started up as the Commander started to speak.

"Don't be sore now, Doctor Cane," he said to me. "This is something neither you nor I can fight. The Tribunal is beyond us," he said shrugging his shoulders.

"How can you just accept that?" I asked.

"There's nothing to accept or not accept," Commander Bryant said moving towards the stairs down into my mind. "Come on, Doctor Cane. We don't have much time."

"You know as well as I that we have as much time as we need. What do you all need inside of my mind?" I asked

"Your enlightenment, Doctor Cane. The Tribunal has asked for it," the Commander answered.

"I don't understand," I said.

"I don't either, but it really doesn't matter. Come now, Doctor Cane. Off we go," the Commander said standing at the top of the stairs leading down into my mind. He knew that another step could not be taken without him.

I wanted to stand firm and go nowhere, but I knew I could not. Down the steps we went.

Humming birds floated by in the hundreds, appearing from the bottom of the stairs. I marched down listening to the footsteps of the Commander echo against the stone walls on either side of us. *Miles Davis's 'Kind of Blue'* shuffled a return from around the corner, as Mile's horn pierced through our eardrums. Stevie had ceased to play at some point. As we approached what I knew to be the bottom, and came to the door of my mind, I paused and looked back at the Commander.

"Here we go, Doctor Cane," he said to me smiling.

The door into my mind appeared to be just as I had seen it last, ordinary and unassuming with green paint chipping off of it. It reminded me of the door to the backyard of the house I grew up in. I felt myself transport back to those first beginning years. The soft breeze of spring washed over me, knocking away all anxiety and fear that had bundled into my belly over the last two decades. Freedom was just beyond this door.

"Shall we open it, Doctor Cane?" The Commander asked me. Smiling his signature grin, the Commander gestured toward the golden doorknob. "Please, Doctor Cane. Time is of the essence."

"Let's go ahead and get this over with," Sifu Ping said from behind us both.

I turned around and saw my teacher sitting on the 3rd to the last step. His feet planted firmly, staring at us with his elbows on his knees, chin in his hands.

"I'm afraid," I said aloud to Sifu Ping. Commander Bryant could not see him. I knew this but it mattered not.

"Come now, Doctor Cane," the Commander responded. "Just a walk through the forest, like we did in mine."

"I'm not sure what is beyond this door," I said to the Commander turning my gaze upon him. My eyes were angry looking at him. I could do nothing to fake the funk I smelt drifting from this man I had thought for a moment was my friend.

"Don't forget," Sifu Ping said softly in my mind. "We are in your mind. You're in control of what happens."

I nodded my head in understanding and reached my hand to the golden doorknob attached to the weathered green door leading into my mind.

A creak sounded from the hinges after I twisted the knob and pushed the door open. A gust of wind grabbed ahold of the green door and forcibly pulled it open. I watched as my weight pulled forward followed by a vacuum pressure that pulled me from my chest, lifting me from my feet. I looked to the side at Commander Bryant and saw from his face that he was being sucked in too. Blackness overcame my screen and I heard the door slam shut.

A faint light appeared. What started out as a small dot ahead of me, grew into a massive blinding white light that I tried to resist to no avail. Once it surrounded the Commander and me, we were floating in an empty dark space with no sound.

No sound was good. Calm overcame me and I knew I was no longer in my own mind. In a blink, the scene of the fiery highway appeared before us. The Crimson Knight stood poised and ready to attack. Unsheathing his giant sword dripping with the blood of countless foes, the Crimson Knight with lightning speed swung the blade down upon me. Sifu Ping appeared in front of me, absorbing the impact and the sword sliced my teacher from right shoulder to left hip. Blood erupted from the massive wound and he collapsed onto me.

With my teacher's body upon my own, I watched as the Crimson Knight removed the giant blade from Sifu Ping and readied itself for another attack. Pushing the body of my teacher from my own, I jabbed at my thigh where the diamond scalpel was sewn into the skin, ripping the surgical instrument from my leg. The pain was excruciating, but not bad enough to slow down the one chance I knew I had. As the Crimson Knight began the arc of another strike, I tossed the diamond scalpel directly into the black eye hold of its armor helmet. As I felt the blade leave my fingertips, I knew I had won in the duel against the Fire Demon's slave.

The diamond scalpel stabbed into the eye hole of the Crimson Knight and it let out a gigantic scream. Bursting my ear drums, I felt the presence of the Commander approaching from behind me. Dropping to my knees and rolling forward onto my back I dodged the attack I had not known was coming. I heard the clank of metal onto the stone ground and pounced onto my feet, turning one hundred eight degrees. Commander Bryant held in his hands a large lance that I knew not from where he had obtained. With the blade end of the lance upon the ground, the Commander looked at me smiling.

"I'm gonna rip that smile off your face," I said to him, smiling my own sadistic grin. I had my teacher's blood on my lips and licked them clean, savoring the moment of calm he and I were in. The Commander let out a grunt that became a yell as his body burst forward with speed I could barely comprehend with my vision. I felt myself falling to the side and my feet leaving the ground. A drift of wind echoing off the blade of the lance Commander Bryant wielded brushed past, centimeters from my face.

I fell onto the withering body of the Crimson Knight and pulled the Diamond Scalpel from the eye hold of its armored helmet. A red eyeball was attached to the tip of the surgeon's instrument. Rolling to the side, I barely dodged the Commander's second strike. Holding up the diamond scalpel, the Crimson Knight's fiery eye stared at me. I darted the blade into my open mouth and put the eye inside. Chewing and swallowing, I shook with disgust as I felt the organ slide down my throat and into my stomach.

From my mouth I extended my elbow outward toward Commander Bryant and launched the diamond scalpel I received from Sifu Ping into the neck of the Commander, as he began to lower the lance upon me in a death blow. Again, I won the duel. With the lance over his head, the Commander smiled one last time before falling backwards. Blood drained from his neck and a pool of blood quickly gathered stretching out from his head. I sat in the same position as when I threw the diamond scalpel with my arm extended and my fingers dangling down in follow through. Swish was all I could think.

Darkness overtook me.

I found myself back in the loading room, looking at myself. Through self-thought therapy, I was able to remove myself in order to prevent from splitting into two personalities. This was the final level to be obtained; I was now the master of my own mind. I smiled at myself and nodded my head towards my own image.

"It's time to wake up," the other version of me said. And thus, I did.

Father Clementine was the face that greeted me. I was cuffed and being disconnected from the thought therapy virtual reality device. I glanced to my left and saw Commander Bryant, eyes wide open staring dead at the ceiling. Blood dripped from his mouth onto the white furry rug.

"I must say, Doctor Cane," Father Clementine said to me. "You certainly put up a good fight."

I stared at him saying nothing.

"Unfortunately, your story must end here," he said.

I smiled and shook my head in disagreement.

"No," I said. "It's only just begun."

"If that's what you want to believe. I admire your tenacity, however, I'm sure you know the law of this country. You will be put to death for going against the Tribunal," Father Clementine said motioning for the agents that were on either side to take me away. I have been in this cell ever since that day.

I'm afraid the ink is running dry from my feather, and it is time for me to move on to my next life. I say to thee, reading this letter, continue to fight. Always stay vigilant and be prepared for the Fire Demon lurking in the subconscious of our minds, whatever it may look like. Waiting and ready at every moment, for the opportune instant to strike. As long as one is observant, good will always prevail over evil. Never give up. The Tribunal will one day be no more.

- *Dr. Cane*

End

11/12/2018 – 03/30/2019

## AUTHOUR'S BIO

Stanley Ish is from the low end of the South Side - Chicago, Illinois. The great grandson of American Actress and contralto vocalist, Etta Moten Barnett. And, great grandson of Claude Barnett, founder of the first international news agency for black newspapers, The Associated Negro Press. Stanley was born and raised SGI Buddhist and has lived in both China and Japan studying the languages of both countries. An alum of Soka University of America, Stanley currently lives in Los Angeles with his partner.

www.ingramcontent.com/pod-product-compliance
Lightning Source LLC
Chambersburg PA
CBHW020019030726
47499CB00007B/2181